for Darby, Elliot,

& Pugnacious

... who believe

Order this book online at www.trafford.com
or email orders@trafford.com

Most Trafford titles are also available at major online book retailers.

Printed in Victoria, BC, Canada.

ISBN: 978-1-4269-3390-5 (sc)

ISBN: 978-1-4269-3510-7 (e-book)

*Our mission is to efficiently provide the world's finest, most comprehensive book publishing
service, enabling every author to experience success. To find out how to publish your book, your
way, and have it available worldwide, visit us online at www.trafford.com*

Trafford rev. 5/25/2010

 www.trafford.com

North America & international
toll-free: 1 888 232 4444 (USA & Canada)
phone: 250 383 6864 ♦ fax: 812 355 4082

Goblin

Tales

A collection of short stories

from the world of fantasy

by

David Kier

Books by David Kier:

Jody

Ravenscroft

The Door to the Shadows

Goblin Tales

Pathways of Learning

PROLOGUE

The following stories were discovered in a hollowed-out tree in a place known to goblins as their "Sacred Grove." There is no way of knowing when these stories were written, though severe fading of the ink and parchment, plus extreme weathering, suggest they are at least a hundred years old. Some of the stories were found in tact; others have survived only as tattered fragments, and are not included here.

The discovery has sparked considerable interest, and has inspired intensive investigation by academics and non-academics alike. The stories have been well received by young *and* old, but present an interesting puzzle -- for none of them has a clearly recognizable author. Questions, therefore, abound: are they the work of a single person? At the same time? Or were they written, by one or more authors, over a long period of time?

Many goblin scholars believe the stories have multiple authorship. But by goblins? Some other faerie folk? Or someone else altogether?

Most reject that last possibility, for it is unlikely that anyone but a goblin (or other faerie folk) would be able to compose such intricate, and occasionally provocative, tales.

In any event, the reader is asked to consider all of that... and to keep an open mind.

1.

Scholars find little controversy in the first tale. Goblin historians are agreed that its theme (why we are here) is a universal one. "Life," to cite an ancient goblin adage, "is a testing arena," and the first tale clearly shows that.

As for it being a tale involving dwarfs, instead of goblins -- that, understandably, has drawn some criticism. One noted goblin scholar (Tal) has gone so far as to say that it shows "how confused and uncertain" dwarfs are, as opposed to goblins. Serri, on the other hand, disagrees. "We must not lose sight," she argues, "of the fact that there are few real differences between goblins and the dwarfs."

Like all the stories that follow, consensus is unlikely. Each reader must determine his or her own meaning.

"Mortimer"

Mortimer was late. All his life, he had been late: late coming into the world, late learning how to walk and talk, late learning the Ways of his people. Not even the most sympathetic soul ever credited Mortimer with being on time for *anything!*

It's not that he *tried* to be late. Mortimer would *never* do that. If nothing else, he was the epitome of thoughtfulness and consideration. It's just that... well, that was his way.

"His special talent," the other dwarfs musingly called it. "Special curse," *he* called it, when he wasn't too embarrassed to think about it. "Why, he'll be late for his own passing!" was a remark frequently heard in his neighborhood.

None of this was said nastily, for how could *anyone* look into that radiant, apple-cheeked face and be less than loving of Mortimer? Still, it did touch a tender and very sensitive spot every time he heard it.

Oh, how I wish I were different! He tried and he tried -- but no matter how hard he tried, somehow he was always late. It would have been better, he often grumbled, if he hadn't tried at all!

Poor Mortimer: frustrated and overwhelmed and teased by his friends... and he had *lots* of friends... all because of his "special talent."

Now he was late again, for the most important day of his life: the confirmation and celebration of his coming of age.

Of course.

He was all frenetic motion, as his tiny legs propelled him through the dark Wood. His lungs took in and puffed out large, rapid gulps of air as he worried his chunky little body to the dwarfs' most sacred place.

He arrived just in time to see the Elders returning scrolls and scepters to their robes. They were preparing to leave.

Of course.

"Wait!" shouted the horrified little dwarf through a voice that was not unlike the squeak of a mouse. "Please don't go!"

The shout got the attention of the five masked and be-robed figures. As one, they looked with quiet sadness (disapproval?) into the eyes of the panting and exhausted truant. A brown-bearded dwarf in a green ceremonial robe spoke first, and forcefully.

"You are late, Mortimer. A minute more and we would have left, and you would have missed the rites. Do you know what that means?"

Indeed he did, and for once Mortimer was not tardy... with a reply.

"Yes, m'lord, I do. I would forfeit my coming of age and be cast out of the clan." He shuddered at the thought.

"As it is," continued an Elder in a silver robe, "you *are* here, so we shall begin. But be advised: we are not pleased." The reproach was delivered firmly. Mortimer lowered his head in understanding.

After a deep sigh, the silver-robed Elder continued.

"Very well. We will now test you on your worthiness for passage into adulthood. Are you ready?"

"Yes, m'lord," he squeaked.

The Elder nodded, and turned to a blue-robed companion who stood off to his left.

"Mortimer, what is the most important thing in life?"

Mortimer gulped hard as he struggled to push an answer from a mouth gone dry as cotton.

"Why ... the most important thing in life ... the most important thing ..."

"Answer the question while we still have breath in our bodies," chided a golden-robed Elder.

"Yes, m'lord, at once. The most important thing is the ... caring for one' s family and clan?"

"You answer the question with a question?" said the green-robed interrogator with an icy blast. "Are you asking, or do you know?"

Sweat began to form in tiny beads on Mortimer's forehead. His pulse was beating loudly. He gulped again.

"Yes, m'lord. The most important thing ... is the caring for one's family and clan."

"Of the two," asked the golden-robed Elder rapid-fire, "if that is your answer, which would you choose first?" The Elders riveted cold stares at the scared little dwarf.

"Why... they're both important," he answered in a voice that was losing ground to panic.

"Yes, yes, we *know* that. But a choice *must* be made. Which of them do you choose?"

Fear was now racing helter-skelter along Mortimer's spine. The beads of sweat were now no longer tiny. Indeed, his whole face felt like a cascading waterfall.

Choose? Which one? But how? He loved his family *and* his clan. For that matter, he loved *all* the clans of the Wood. He could not decide, and allowing for his well-known honesty to carry the day he said so.

"I... cannot choose. They are *both* important to me."

"*What!*" asked a red-robed Elder indignantly. "*Can't* choose!"

"Perhaps," interrupted the silver-robed Elder, to restore calm, "young Mortimer can answer that in another way." He looked at the dwarf with a modicum of compassion (or pity?).

"Let us put this another way. You say you cannot choose. Very well: but are *those* the most important things in life?"

"Yes, m'lord," Mortimer replied, with some confusion. "Surely, they are."

"Some would say," the same Elder continued, "that the most important thing in life is oneself. How would you answer that?"

A trap? But no; Elders are above that. They do not trap. But if it is ... It was no use. Mortimer could only say what he believed. He phrased his reply with the sweat streaming down his face.

"I do not know. I do not know because I am young and yet unlearned in the Ways of the world. I cannot say that I am most important, because I do not know. Nor can I choose between my family and my clan, because I do not know how. I am sorry, m'lord. I just do not know."

There was a short pause - though it seemed infinitely longer to poor Mortimer. The silver-robed Elder stepped off to one side and spoke in hushed tones with the others. It did not take them long to reach a verdict.

"We hear your answers," said the silver-robed Elder again, "and can now respond to them.

"You say that you can't choose between your family and your clan; that you are unsure as to what is the most important thing in life. I must tell you that your uncertainty in this matter is most grave and worrisome."

Mortimer was all empty inside, and waited with no enthusiasm whatsoever for the world to swallow him up, for the Elders to fail him and banish him from the Wood. He didn't have long to wait.

"Worrisome, yes, but commendable. The test of maturity, Mortimer, can be in *not* always knowing. The same thing goes for your indecision in choosing between two equally important choices. Only the immature and the unwise rush to judgment regarding that which is paramount. So it is no great sin *not* to choose between your family and your clan. Nor is it a sin to say so. In fact, we are all agreed that it is laudatory *not* to leap to a choice. For once, *not* rushing to something works in your favor!"

Mortimer was dumbstruck. It was all he could do to get his mouth working again.

"You mean ... you mean you're not going to cast me out of the Wood? I've ... passed?"

The silver-robed Elder could not suppress a series of chuckles.

"No, no, young Mortimer, we are most assuredly *not* going to cast you out. And yes, you have 'passed.'

"You see, the test of passage is as much in the heart as it is in the head, and your responses were as sincere and honest as any we have heard in a very long time. They remind us, in fact, of another young dwarf, who, many years ago, answered largely as you have just done. But he *was* cast out for his honesty. Thereupon, he proved himself, under the greatest duress and the most trying of circumstances, to be every bit as worthy as the most cocksure of his peers. So much so, in fact, that by his example the Elders changed the testing to reward such budding maturity. And that dwarf? He became my good right arm and my dearest friend."

At that, the silver-robed Elder removed the ceremonial mask that hid his features to reveal himself to be Graemore, wizard of Delvin Wood. And out of the shadows came the familiar visage of his good and trusted friend.

"Uncle Clarence!" Mortimer cried in surprise.

The Elders now disbursed, leaving Mortimer, Graemore, and Clarence alone in the Wood. After a little while it was time, too, for them to go their various ways.

"Don't forget," the wizard and the uncle yelled as they left, "to join us at the Keep on the morrow for a proper celebration. Don't be late!"

Just as buoyantly, if a little sheepishly, Mortimer replied: "Don't worry, I won't be late!"

And, of course -- he was!

2.

The second tale elicited no controversy whatsoever. "Obviously," commented Serri," this elder tale comes directly from our past, and without coloration." She pointed to honor and duty - always esteemed by goblins - and especially the paternalism that one finds in so much goblin lore.

"Equally important," said Tal, "are the references to ritual. Being a *Quellspirer* is a noble undertaking, and we can date that title easily to half a millennium ago."

"Yes," agreed Serri, "but I am not sure of the ceremony referred to as *Sun Crest.* Is that a true rendering, or just something added to embellish the tale?"

"I think I can answer that." The new voice belonged to Nicomaides, the wisest of the goblins, whose ancestry (it was rumored) dated to the Time of Promise, more than a thousand years ago.

"There was a ceremony," he continued, "which, in the elder tongue, was called *Tarrin.* One translation, as I render it, could be 'Sun Crest.'"

"Then the story was not necessarily written by a goblin," answered Tal.

"Perhaps not," replied Nicomaides. "But let's leave its authorship for a later discussion. Rather, let us do what the Elders have charged us with: to study and evaluate the *substance* of the tales."

"Jeremy"

Cedric the goblin was worried. It was his task - indeed, his *honor* - to watch over the younger goblins of the Shire who lived and studied at the Master's school, deep in the Sparkling Forest. It was a job he had done with pride and joy for more than half of his 150 years -- for he was not only the young goblins' protector, he was also their teacher. He took much pleasure in instructing the youth of the Wood in forest lore: the language of the trees and the flowers; the philosophies of the foxes, rabbits, and bears. Cedric was proud to be a **Quellspirer:** a Master's Assistant. It was a task he took very seriously. It was as important as life itself.

Yet today Cedric was worried, for Jeremy, one of the Master's pupils, was missing.

He did not know how such a thing could have happened. He had done everything to find the boy. Since the sun first began spilling slices of light and warmth on the dense, majestic grove that was home, he had been asking for help.

Jeremy had not been at *Sun Crest*, the daily gathering of the Master's pupils at daybreak, where they stood in the Ring of Stones and sang their joyful welcome of the star's life-enriching energies. At first Cedric thought Jeremy might have overslept - a minor failing of responsibility, but not enough to warrant concern.

In fact, it was not until mid-day, when the Master's pupils came together once again to thank the Earth for its bounty, the trees for their protective cover, and the flowers for their beauty, that it became clear that Jeremy was truly missing. To miss the greeting to the Sun was one thing, but to miss a *second* celebration was unheard of! So Cedric began making inquiries.

No, said one of the other goblins, he had not seen him all morning. Jeremy? Why, said another, I haven't seen him since Nightcall, the ritualistic thanksgiving for the mantle of darkness that the Great Sky Spirit lovingly provided to protect goblins and others of the Wood.

Now it was late in the day, and Cedric still had not found his charge.

Where could he be? What could have happened to him? There was a wince of pain, for Jeremy was the smallest of the goblins, and the weakest. If he had wandered too far from the safety of the Wood...

Cedric should have pushed that thought from his mind, but he could not. He was, after all, the **Quellspirer**. His concern grew; he had violated his vow; he had compromised a trust. Worse: of all the Master's pupils, Jeremy was Cedric's favorite: a shy, timid little goblin who always looked at him in awe, through larger-than-life yellow-brown eyes. His rust-colored fur even seemed to shine more when they were together, discussing the world, the universe, or goblin lore.

Maybe it was because Jeremy was an orphan; maybe it was because he saw in Cedric a father figure -- though grandfather or even *great*-grandfather would be more appropriate. Cedric was, after all, a *very* old goblin! Reciprocally, Cedric was drawn to Jeremy, as the son he never had, the continuation of a family line long since expired.

He and Jeremy talked a lot -- for Jeremy was very bright -- and they laughed a lot, and Jeremy had said, amidst the talking and the laughing, that someday he would like to do something nice for his mentor. Cedric smiled warmly at that.

He wasn't smiling now. He was frowning, and looking, frantically, every place where Jeremy might be. The other pupils looked, too. They, likewise, shuddered at the prospect of Jeremy wandering off too far...

And the Master! He will surely be enraged. What will he do, even if Jeremy escapes the smallest harm? The Master is a powerful figure, the eldest and most learned of goblins. His punishment would be fearsome!

At this moment, though, Cedric cared not at all about that, for if anything *were* to happen to Jeremy, no punishment could ever be as big as that which Cedric would inflict upon himself.

My son... he absently mumbled to himself - before he caught himself in a moment of shock. *No,* he groaned; *he is* not *my son; he is a pupil of the Master, and he is in my charge. That is all. I have no son, no family...*

Desperately, he kept searching. He asked the residents of the forest. He gathered the rabbits and the foxes and the badgers, and beseeched them to search the bottom lands. He asked the marmots and the squirrels to comb the trees. He asked the great white owl and the lowly red sparrow to search the skies. *Find Jeremy,* he implored of them in their own special language.

Find him and guide him safely home...

Yet when the day came to an end, one by one, the beasts and the birds of the Wood had found nothing.

Darkest imaginings welled up inside of Cedric as he listlessly watched the Master's other pupils gather at the Ring of Stones to greet another night. Tonight his mind and heart were elsewhere, so the customary melodious offering of thanks wound sound hollow. Spirits were very low, indeed.

An hour after the Master's pupils had retired to their tree-beds, Cedric was yet keen to the sounds of the night; still lost in his misery and his despair; wondering where he might look next.

Jeremy, oh Jeremy: where are you?

Then, just as his heart had sunk to its lowest ebb, Cedric heard a sharp rustling noise behind him. When he turned to detect its cause, there, just beyond the Ring of Stones, stood Jeremy!

The young goblin was smiling... but that lasted only the briefest of moments, for in the blink of an eye he saw that Cedric had been terribly worried.

"Jeremy!" exclaimed the old goblin, almost falling over his feet in his rush to get to his charge -- not to punish him, but to embrace him. But in that instant he stopped, for the Master appeared at his side.

"All is well, Cedric," boomed the mellow voice that belonged to the wisest of the goblins. "Young Jeremy has been with me since yesterday eve; he has been in no jeopardy."

"But... but why wasn't I told? I've ... we've been worried sick that something had happened to him."

"I'm sorry," said Jeremy in a way that left no doubt as to his sincerity.

"I didn't think you'd be so worried. I'm sorry."

Before Cedric could reply, the Master spoke.

"The fault lies not with Jeremy, but with me. The lad came to me with a problem and I fear we were overlong in resolving it. So it is *I* who should ask forgiveness."

Cedric sputtered out a weak reply.

"You? Oh, no. You are the Master; it must have been my fault..."

"Nonsense! Even Masters can make mistakes - so let's hear no more of this!"

Reluctantly, he obeyed. He said no more about blame or responsibility. Rather, curiosity led him to ask about Jeremy's problem.

"Oh, that," answered the Master, trying to slough it off as a matter of little consequence.

"Well," snorted Cedric, "whatever it was, *surely* it could not have been so unimportant that you wouldn't have told me... or that you would have been gone for almost an entire day!"

Cedric was hurt, and it showed.

"Oh, but I think it was," said the Master, chuckling just a little bit under his breath.

"Well, then?" asked Cedric.

"It seems our young friend here has found someone he likes very much, and wondered what our laws were, regarding adoption."

Cedric's heart sank. *That someone is very, very lucky.*

"It's not the kind of thing that comes up every day, " the Master continued, "so I had to consult the ancient scrolls."

"And what is the law?" asked Cedric through tightly-pursed lips.

"The law, as I read it, is that adoption can be initiated by either the child or the parent-to-be. All that is required is the request by the one to the Master, followed by mutual consent. It seems that our boy here is very fond of someone in the Wood, and wishes to carry on his good name."

"I see," said Cedric, feeling even more envious, if also even lower than before.

"So, now it is done --- or half done, for Jeremy has asked me, and I have approved."

"And?" asked Cedric.

"And now," said the Master, "the rest is up to you."

Cedric was stunned.

"Me? I don't understand..."

"It's up to you..."

Jeremy interrupted.

"It's up to you, because *you* are the one whose name I wish to bear. It's *your* love that means so much to me!"

Once again, Cedric was stunned.

"But... I am an old man, a very old man..."

"Nonsense," said Jeremy. "You may be old in years, but you're young in spirit and heart. I have learned so much from you and wish to learn more. Will you be my father?"

Cedric could no longer stand. He sought with his hands a rock to sit upon, while he waited for his brain to catch up with his thumping heart.

Father? Me? An old man, with no family of my own?... and that was true. No family; no one to call his son. A voice within him cried out to say no: this is a foolish idea. Seconds later, he yielded to another voice.

"Yes," he answered through a dry mouth. "Yes, Jeremy, I would like very much to be your father."

As the two goblins -- one very young, the other now not so very old -- embraced in love and friendship, the Master of the goblins took his place at the Ring of Stones and rippled with laughter.

"So, Jeremy, not only do you now have a father ... you've got a *grand*father, too!"

3.

The third story caused considerable puzzlement, for it contained neither goblins, dwarfs, nor *any* of the faerie folk who lived in the goblins' world. That led Serri to observe that "it was most likely written by a goblin, but as pure fantasy -- like giving a hedgehog a voice so that he might speak of how he's treated in the forest."

"Hedgehogs there may be," argued Tal, "but *flying horses!* Why would a goblin -- or *any* faerie folk -- choose such a ridiculous and improbable creature?"

"Perhaps," replied Nicomaides, "it was done with no more mystery than to show how free *any* winged creature is. It could be nothing more than a translation error: instead of a "flying horse," the author may have intended it to be an eagle, or a condor."

"But one that *talks!*" Clearly, Tal was beside himself.

"Once again," Nicomaides countered, "we are quibbling about form, when we should be discussing substance."

"I have just one question," said Serri. "If this is just a fantasy - and I admit it feels that way to me - what, then, is 'man'? We don't even have a word for such a creature. What *is* man?"

"Cleotaxes"

Cleotaxes loved to fly. To soar through the azure skies, to leap through patchy white clouds, to glide a path that would take her closer, ever closer to the sun's energizing rays -- oh, she so loved the warmth she got from that golden ball of life!

It was a game of riding the thermals without going too far, without getting too close to the sun and burning up, as had happened not so long ago to silly old Icarus.

But Icarus was a fool. A man who dared to fly - *yes, quite a fool,* she thought, as she threw back her proud head and absorbed the wind and the sun in her snow white mane. How ludicrous: a man trying to be like the winged horses of Anacreon!

The day was a good one for flying, and Cleotaxes reveled in it. The sky was clear and crisp. Summer was waning, and that meant she'd soon be getting her winter coat -- a darker, thicker covering that would carry her through the rains and snows that all too soon would visit her world. The thought, however, was just a momentary one, a minor, unpleasant distraction on such an otherwise perfect day. Two climbs later it was all but forgotten, and Cleotaxes was doing what she enjoyed more than anything else: flying free, high and wide, without a care in the world.

Toward day's end, she came to a long, low valley she had never seen. Flying horses are extraordinarily curious creatures; absolutely *nothing* escapes their attention. So she spread wide her long tapered wings to swoop down for a closer look. As she did so, something on a small ridge caught her eye. It glistened -- whatever "it" was -- not unlike the reflection of the sun upon a smooth rock (which is what she thought it was). In the wink of an eye, though, she knew it was not: the glisten grew and diminished and grew again. There also were colors - reds and yellows and blues and browns. This required a much closer inspection!

She angled gracefully toward the glistening, stretched out her long sleek body for the dive, and glided effortlessly onto the ridge. She touched down with her feathered hooves just six feet from the source of her curiosity.

That produced quite a shock -- for the glistening was a person. It appeared as if out of nowhere, like a sorcerer. Which, as it turned out, it was. Cleotaxes was startled, but not afraid. Winged horses, you see, are the favorites of the gods and are immortal. Just the same, she was surprised, and said so, to the long-robed, white-haired figure who stood before her.

"You need not be alarmed, freest of the free, for I am Aramcarr, sorcerer of the Temple of Saphos, and am charged this day by our Lady Hera to meet with you and bid your assistance."

Immortals are not easily impressed, but a request from the highest of all the goddesses -- and the patron of winged horses, no less -- sufficed. Cleotaxes was impressed.

"What assistance does our Lady require of me?" she asked, with perhaps too much humility. Sorcerers, even those who are not immortal, are not fools, and Aramcarr knew full well that winged horses are famous for their arrogance and their aloofness.

"Your task," Aramcarr slowly replied with sternness in his voice, "is to take a message to a remote and somewhat inaccessible place."

"It shall be done, master sorcerer. What is the message?"

"The message you will hear in good time."

"But how..."

"You shall hear the message in good time," interrupted Aram-carr, "after you have delivered the message-bearer."

Cleotaxes' eyes opened wide. *Message-bearer?* Another surprise in a day of surprises!

"And who might this 'message-bearer' be?" she asked icily, her sizable curiosity tinged with just a hint of sarcasm.

"This is the message-bearer." Aramcarr pointed to a small form that now walked timidly into view from a crag beneath the ridge.

"A man-child!" she snorted, her eyes absolutely incredulous at the sight. "A puny man-child, to accompany me on a mission for the gods!"

"To ride with you," the sorcerer smoothly corrected.

This was more than an immortal could bear!

"No man-creature has ever ridden me -- *no* creature has!"

"Well, then," chuckled Aramcarr, enjoying the disgruntlement, "today shall be doubly noteworthy. This will be a first."

Flying horses do not breathe fire -- that is reserved for dragons, of course -- but if ever a horse wanted to do so, it was now. Cleotaxes was so furious that her nostrils verily flared. Hot breath came billowing forth (but no fire). The man-child, who had cowered at the sight of the wondrous steed, had moved not an inch and said nothing. He was not an immortal, and doubtless wondered at that moment if he would reach the next minute, let alone the completion of the mission!

Once again, Aramcarr interceded to bring order out of chaos, holding up a stern right hand to bid silence in the mounting din.

"The boy, here" -- and he was clearly no more than that -- "is named Milo, and he, and he alone, bears the message. Know that, for that is all you will hear from me. Take him to his destination, and see to it that no harm comes to him."

Cleotaxes huffed and fumed for several seconds more... but, of course, she acceded to the sorcerer's command. She dared not go against the gods!

"All right," she grumbled, "climb onto my back, man-child," she said with considerable contempt, "and we shall go. Where is it that I am to take him, sorcerer?"

"To Olympus, my friend. You are to take him to the seat of the gods."

Cleotaxes' gasp was audible enough for anyone to hear. Olympus! Home of the gods -- home of Hera, and Zeus and all the rest! To say that this was an honor was to underscore the obvious. Rarely had anyone -- and *never* Cleotaxes -- been to the majestic throne-hall of the gods. This was *indeed* a day of surprises!

"I suggest," added Aramcarr, seeing the objection disappear from her eyes, "that you begin immediately. Your task is huge, and time is of the essence."

With that, the great horse lowered her head so that the timid man-child -- who still had not uttered a sound -- could take hold of her mane and ease himself upon her sturdy back. In seconds, they were on their way.

The journey was long, and many leagues had to be counted, but that was not difficult for Cleotaxes. The difficulty was in accommodating the human... for him it *did* seem like a long journey. Not of making him comfortable - that never occurred to her - but of simply getting accustomed to the presence of such a pitiful being. Gods or no, it was a most loathsome idea. *Maybe he will fall off*, she leered as she sped through the late afternoon sky. *It could happen to anyone. Surely, the gods would not hold her responsible for* that!

Then she caught herself: they *would* hold her accountable. So pride had to be swallowed; she not only had to go to Olympus, but she had to make sure that no harm came to the human. It was almost too much.

"Why do you dislike me?" That was the first thing the man-child had said, and it was so unexpected that it caused Cleotaxes to wobble perceptibly in her flight. *So it speaks*, she said under her breath. *Too bad; I had hoped it would be mute!* She chose to ignore the question.

"I'm sorry that I displease you so," he tried again. "I don't wish to offend you, nor do I wish to displease the gods. I hope you understand."

After several leagues of flying, during which Cleotaxes' silence was almost loud enough to shatter mountains, she passed the time thinking about what would be so important to summon her to the throne of the gods. Finally it struck her -- with some shock -- that she was merely the *carrier* of the one who bore the 'message' ... an immortal made subservient to a mere human ... and a pitiful one at that.

Have the gods taken leave of their senses?

Happily, she reproached herself, she had not said that aloud. The gods, as everyone knows, have big ears! Still, her wonder grew. Her resentment of the creature certainly did not diminish.

At long last - or so it seemed - she was upon her goal: clouded, shrouded Mt. Olympus was in view, and within minutes... as darkness was enveloping the world below her in a cloak of gray ...the journey would be at an end and the mystery would be solved.

The large winged horse thrust downward, and in an instant had stretched her long white body at the cluster of thick clouds, beneath which, as legend recorded it, resided the pantheon of gods, ruled with finality and justice by Zeus, lord of the heavens.

In a wink they were there, the man-child still clinging tightly to the horse's mane. Cleotaxes trod several paces to the palace, and stopped. Waiting at the portal was Hera.

"Welcome to Olympus, faithful steed," announced the goddess in a voice that erased any doubts of those foolish enough to have them that she was, indeed, queen of the gods.

"You are here, proud mare of mares because your story, and the story of all who claim immortality, is about to change."

Change? The word ran wild through her mind. *Change? How?*

"While it is true," continued Hera, "that you have roamed and soared through the skies for as long as there is memory, the times now require other things, other purposes.

"Those who we made -- you among them -- were granted long life, for we, as immortals, anticipated that things would always be the same. In that, we were wrong.

"We did not foresee the day when lesser beings would rise and challenge us. Nor did we expect that once they had begun their rise they would lose interest in us, and have no need of us.

"Well, noble steed, that time has come to pass, and you -- and many of your fellows -- have to change as we have.

"From this day forward there will be no gods -- we will all disappear, except into the ancient and ever-turning memories of the world. That is the will of Cosmos, and to go against it would be to unleash his terrible brother, Chaos, upon the earth.

"But," said Hera very gently, "we do not wish to cause your end. So, we have decided that you will remain, but shorn of your powers, and of your immortality. The Age of Man is beginning, and it shall not require such as you. You will be mortal; you will share the world with Man and will live and die with him.

"You, more than all the beings we have made, will need to learn to share, to be more giving and less selfish, more caring and less independent. You will have no further need of wings, for your freedom, as man's, must know limitations if you are to survive.

"Heed this, though: you, more than your brothers the Harpies, dragons, and the unicorns, can work with man, be his friend, his companion. We have seen this, and it will be so.

"You must make this effort, and all the world will benefit. Do that, and you will do us proud."

That was it. An instant later Hera was gone, the throne-hall of the gods was gone -- all was gone. It was as if nothing or no one had ever been there.

Cleotaxes was stunned. After a brief time, and in a moment of wild panic, she sought to test the truth of the awful tale she had been told. But to no avail. The strong wings she had used to get airborne and to freedom were gone. She was no longer a being of the sky.

After what seemed an eternity of self-remorse and melancholy she felt the presence of another. It was the man-child, Milo, and he was standing beside her, stroking her nose.

"I'm sorry you have heard this. I'm sorry that this had to happen. I'm sorry, too, that your destiny was riding upon your back this day, and that I was the messenger of that destiny."

Cleotaxes looked down for the first time at the human, and caught the fullness of the misery that sat in its eyes. It was genuine and all-consuming, and for the first time she felt something she had never known before: compassion. This, she thought, quietly in her grief; this, then, is mortality.

"Be as friends," Hera had commanded, "and you shall do us proud... do us proud... do us proud...."

"I know," wept Milo, drying the tears from his reddened eyes. "I know what freedom has meant to you, how heart-breaking it must be to part with it. I know it very well indeed."

"How could you know about freedom?" asked Cleotaxes with a tone that was hard and sharp.

Milo sighed. "Have you ever heard of a man named Icarus?"

"Yes," she snorted. "He was a fool of a man who thought he could fly!"

Milo looked down and then up again into the horse's eyes.

"Icarus was my father."

Like a cover of darkness lifting, Cleotaxes understood. Freedom was for all to try. She and other immortals had it, as a gift, only to lose it when their immortality vanished. Now she must share the search with others - like Man - and learn what freedom *can* be, and how to keep it.

Yes, she understood. So she lowered her head, made a gesture not unlike affection, and walked with the man-child down the mountain and to a new beginning.

4.

About the only thing that the three scholars agreed upon in the following tale was that there *are* gnomes in their world. Beyond that, the tale was all but dismissed.

"Gibberish," snorted Tal, "it's pure and simple gibberish. Going off to another planet, indeed!"

"I agree," seconded Serri. "After all: as all goblins know, there is *only* this world. There are no others. This we have known since time immemorial."

"Yes," replied Nicomaides, in a cautionary manner. "But why, then, was the tale written? What purpose does it serve to tell of a place if it cannot possibly exist?"

Tal and Serri stared stupidly at the wisest of the goblins, believing, in that moment, that he had lost his mind.

"Myron"

Myron was confused. The rain was like shimmering spears as it beat down on the bare rocks and raced higgledy-piggledy into reddish-brown gullies. Not that he hadn't seen rain before: Myron came from a place where rainy days out-numbered sunny ones. It was just that he had expected to materialize somewhere else: in a place that never knew rain, nor any kind of moisture, for that matter.

Myron, you see, was a traveler: a very special kind of traveler. He would think a place in his mind and then, after performing some mental gymnastics, would be there.

It was a convenient way to travel, to say the least, but it could also have its drawbacks... as he had just discovered.

The funny thing was that he was apparently the only one who

could do this; still more remarkable was the fact that no one else *knew* that he could do it. Well, almost no one. When he was six, he discovered this gift (if "gift" was the right word) purely by accident. One bright summer day he had displeased his overbearing father, and was loudly informed, from a distant part of the house, that he was about to be punished. Myron was not at all pleased with that prospect, so he did a thing that most boys and girls since the beginning of time have done: he wished he were somewhere else.

Only for him something quite extraordinary happened: he got his wish!

In an instant (however long that may be) he was alongside a stream in the forest near his home, listening with satisfaction and relief to the pacifying sounds of gurgling water and the chirping of birds in the trees. Later, after he had wished himself back home, his father had bellowed forth nebulous (and not so nebulous) tirades about where he had hidden himself, where he had got to, and other such yammerings that disguised the fact that he could not figure out where in the world his son had gone - or how. As a consequence, he forgot about the beating he had planned to give.

Myron couldn't explain what had saved him. Six years old is a fragile time, one at which most little boys are just barely distinguishable from an egg plant. It is not an age noted for its intellectual ferment. All that he "knew" was that he had a way - if he could replicate it - for escaping the wrath of an outraged parent. So he spent a lot of moments that summer down by the stream; and Myron's father grew more and more flummoxed and confounded, as he kept wondering where his swift-footed son kept going!

After a while, Myron discovered that not only could he get out of a beating, he could get out of a lot of other things that were similarly displeasing ...like when his kiss-happy cousin Tara came visiting, around harvest time. When his parents could not explain why Myron wasn't there to greet her, cousin Tara huffed off indignantly, vowing never to return. That pleased Myron very much.

As he got older -- ah, the advantage of age -- he made more of his "gift." He got out of many things he did not want to do, and one day in high school he learned -- to his shock and surprise -- that he could go literally just about *any place* he wanted, not just that favorite watering hole in the woods. One day, for instance, when he was suffering overmuch from one of the valley's oppressive heat spells, he wished he were at the North Pole. And, poof! he was. Another thought later and he was back in the midsummer's heat... for he had not been suitably dressed for all that cold!

After that, the sky was the limit -- and then one day in college he reached out and discovered that the sky was *not* the limit.

Truth to tell, Myron was very lucky -- the kind of luck that could kill as well as help -- and he was smart enough to understand that there were some places in the known universe to which a human could will himself that were dangerous. So Myron did not attempt the folly of willing his body to the moon's Sea of Tranquility, or to a polar ice cap on Mars, or to one of the icy snowballs of Saturn's famous rings.

Then it hit him one day: what about the *unknown* universe?

The thought hit him like a ton of bricks. Someplace *not* known? Why not? Think of a place: a place without a name; a place with an earth-like atmosphere, an earth-like gravity; and all the rest. A pleasant place, a quiet place, like the forest of his youth. Think of it. And go there. So he did what he always did: and he went.

So there he was, somewhere in that unknown universe, being soaked to the bone and uncomfortable as hell (and, for all he knew, that might just be where he was!).

Confused? Yes! This was *not* what he had willed! So he grumbled once or twice, and said: "very well, let's go back home." He closed his eyes and transported himself back home. Only this time, when he opened his eyes, he was *not* back home. The rain was still soaking him. He had not left!

Confusion now gave way to fear. *Try again. Blink.* The rain still fell. Fear was now losing ground to panic. Again, he tried; again, he failed. And again, and again, and again.

Myron lost all track of time while the terror was taking him over. Maybe he was too tired to succeed right now; maybe.... There had to be an explanation; he just needed time to find it. Meanwhile, he had to get out of this infernal rain.

About two hundred yards away, across some of the bare-faced rocks that seemed to pock-mark this dreary place, he saw a hollowed-out area in a cliff. A cave, perhaps, or at least a cleft in the rock wall. Shelter, in any case. Without another thought on that score, he slogged his way over to it.

It was just high enough for him to enter, if he bent very low. Thankfully, it was deep enough to accommodate him, and protect him from the rain -- which looked like it was never going to let up. As his eyes became accustomed to the darkness he saw that there was no back to the shelter. It was indeed a cave. An animal's lair? He groaned; whatever it was, it would have to do. He thought friendly thoughts... and fell asleep.

When he awoke it was still raining -- harder, or so it seemed. Was this the natural order of things on this planet? Did it rain *all* the time? He got no further with that, for instinct told him that *he was not alone.* Defensively, he turned slowly about and found that he was right. Against one wall, not ten feet away, sat the figure of a gnome.

At least, that was what Myron's half-crazed mind *thought* it was. He stared at it. The gnome was small -- just a bit over four feet tall, when it stood up (*if* it stood). It was dressed all in fur (or the fur was its permanent covering?), with a face that poked out of some of the same stuff. The face had a nose and two eyes. If there was a mouth he couldn't see it. A second or two later the gnome spoke.

"You are well?" it asked, adding yet another surprise to Myron's day of surprises.

"You speak my language?" he responded, instantly aware of how ridiculous that must have sounded. Under the circumstances, though, *anything* was ridiculous in this upside down world!

"Not really," the gnome answered. "Rather, I am just communicating in a way you can understand. I am simply reaching into your mind."

Myron looked closer at the figure. He still could see no mouth. Evidently, the creature was talking to him with its mind.

He struggled to recapture some balance.

"You are of this planet?"

"Oh, no," the gnome replied, the barest hint of what passed for a twinkle appearing in its eyes.

"I am from another place, a more cheerful place -- not such as this."

"You are a... traveler?"

"In a way. Our travelers -- if I understand your meaning -- seek many things: new worlds, new races, new ideas. More correctly, we are collectors."

"Collectors?"

"Yes; we are a race that needs to collect. We are an old race, one that must have new challenges in order to survive."

"That sounds like some members of my race," said Myron.

"Oh, but it is a different matter with us. You see, my race is dying."

"Dying?

"Yes, dying; the sorting out of beings, according to the dictates of the evolutionary process... "

"I understand the term."

"Then," continued the gnome, "you understand the need for that which is new, if only in the hope that a race may find something, somewhere that will help with its continuation."

Myron was about to reply to the gentle-looking alien, when a sudden shock of discovery burst upon him.

"Yes," said the gnome with his mind. "Our meeting on this dis- agreeable planet was no accident. You were summoned."

A gurgle of terror sounded in Myron's throat.

Summoned? How? Why? By whom?

"For the moment," continued the other, "accept what I say is true. Accept, too, that the summoning was done in good faith -- that is your expression for it, yes?" Myron slowly nodded his head.

I hope so!

"How this occurred is not important. Let's just say that I sensed you, reached out and intercepted you. That is why you are here, instead of the pleasant little planet you were seeking."

"What is it that you want of me?"

As Myron asked this, he tried hurriedly to will himself home, away from the gnome. He failed.

"I am sorry, but your ability to teleport has been voided... for the moment, anyway."

"For the moment?"

"Yes. If you will help us, we would be appreciative and generous to a fault."

"And if not?"

"Then," sighed the gnome, "we will reactivate your gift, and you will be able to go about your business."

Myron relaxed for the first time. It was still raining.

"What do you want?"

"We want knowledge: new ideas, philosophies, and the like, for ours is a civilization for whom those things are as food is to yours. Without them we are nothing. We've not found new knowledge in our universe for many, many years... so we are dying."

"You think I can help you -- by giving you ours?"

"Yes, just so. I can reach the tip of your mind only, yet what I find excites me, fills me with wonder. A whole new, alien civilization..."

Alien. Myron had never thought of his own race as "alien." Yet, to someone else it would be. Just as he himself was something of an alien to his own people.

"You see," said the gnome, "you are important because you are unique. You're the only one of your kind who can do what you do."

"Well, if your people can travel where *they* will," Myron interrupted, "why do you need me?"

"Oh, but we can't. You and I are of two different universes, and there are limits to where we can go. We can't go into your universe, though you, for whatever reason, have the ability to come into ours."

"I don't understand. We're talking, you and I, right now, and yet you say our two races can't come together?"

"That is correct. Look more closely and you'll see what I mean."

Myron did look closer, and he saw what the gnome had said. He could see right through him to the cave wall!

"'Yes," the gnome replied, "the visage is a projection. My mind is sending to you from a place far away. The projection is for your convenience, for you to see what we look like, and to assuage your sanity."

After several moments Myron replied.

"All you want is an exchange of knowledge?"

"Yes, that is all. Simply do that and we will both benefit."

"I don't know..."

"You doubt our sincerity," said the gnome, "and our intentions. Very well; I accept that. Put your suspicions aside; look inside *my* mind."

He did. And he beheld a pink world, everywhere a pastoral vista filled with beauty and majesty. On it was a civilization that was the celebration of a vast and beautiful universal spirit, akin to brother-hood (though that was not exactly the right term). It was a world not quite technological, yet not quite rural, either. Rather, it seemed to be a joining of both, into something else. He couldn't perceive it. All he knew was that he wished he could see it for himself. It was the kind of place he'd always dreamed of; that place of peace and harmony that had been the forest when he was a boy. With that thought came an interruption.

"You *can* see it, Myron. Remember: *you* can go between the universes; we cannot. Do what we ask -- share your civilization with us, and we will tell you how to go there."

"But what you want is so much..."

"It is what we need, what we require. Go back, fill your mind with your planet's treasures, and bring them to us. We will be waiting."

"Then... I am free to go?"

"Yes, of course; our hold on you was only temporary. Only until we had a chance to convey to you our good will. You may leave at any time."

"And if I choose not to return?"

"Then," whispered the gnome, "that is your decision. We cannot go into your universe, we cannot come after you, we cannot get the knowledge ourselves. If you choose to go back and forget us, then we shall die and be forgotten. The choice is yours alone."

Myron sat silent for the longest time, struggling with the gnome's words. *Return to earth...* absorb all of earth's treasures. Only *Myron* could do that. And give those to the gnome and his race? What if their purpose should *not* be "beneficial," but evil? To use the knowledge to launch a terrible invasion, regardless of what the gnome said, and to bring the earth to its knees?

Rubbish; the gnomes could not invade his universe. So what's the harm? And the sharing just might benefit everyone.

After several minutes he gave his answer.

"I will do this. I will return to my planet and do this thing. When shall we meet again?"

"Anytime you wish," answered the gnome. "We 'know' you now: just will yourself to this place again, and one of us will be here."

"And your planet? Will I be able to see your home?"

"Yes, you will. You will indeed."

Myron crossed the length and breadth of his native planet many times in the weeks and months that followed, observing and absorbing earth's myriad achievements, its most noteworthy civilizing features. Then, at the propitious moment, he shut his eyes, willed his mind and his body, and found himself in the presence of a gnome.

Soon thereafter Myron got his wish. He traveled to that alien planet... and never left.

5.

If the elders thought "Myron" was ridiculous, the following story made that one look imminently feasible. To put it mildly, all three goblins were flabbergasted, agreeing unanimously that it was the silliest story they had ever read.

"Socrates"

Socrates had just turned ten thousand years of age when he heard that an alien life force soon would be arriving at the Martian Astronomical station in the Plain of Jars. Despite his great antiquity,

Socrates was fidgety -- acting for all the cosmos like a robot who had been forged only yesterday. That was very uncharacteristic of *any* robot, let alone one of his age!

What distinguished this was the fact that the discovery no longer was a secret. Months ago, the first radio signals from the alien craft had been snared by the enormous radio dishes that jutted up from nearby Mt. Olympus. The dishes dominated the anvil-shaped peak, stretching out over ten square miles and fitting the top of the majestic spire like a huge glove, sending signals well beyond Andromeda and transmitting them instantly back to the ancient and diminutive dishes at Arecibo on distant Earth.

Socrates appreciated the cosmic irony, for the Martian dishes were a thousand times larger than their puny terran counterparts. Their construction had been a colossal undertaking, requiring several centuries of consistent, unrelenting toil. For Socrates that was but a brief moment in his life (if one could properly call the service of a robot a life). For him, it was an easy accomplishment, which he in fact had overseen from its inception. Hence, too, his name, given in the beginning by a long-dead human administrator, whose sense for history was not divorced from his taste for black humor. Here, then, Socrates was "born," named after that philosopher of twelve millennia ago who had espoused human conceptions of the yet-unknown universe in the shadows of that other Mt. Olympus.

As he now reflected on it - which in all honesty he had not done for nearly three hundred years - he couldn't remember whether that administrator was giving him a compliment, or was holding him in contempt. It bothered him that he could not remember.

I must be getting human, he grumbled to himself, *for I am for-getting things -- and a robot never forgets!* What passed for humor raced through his electronic brain: *maybe*, he forced himself to think, *I am becoming senile!*

The peculiar "humanness" that he sensed had been developing, in fact, for several centuries, even antedating the Project (which, in keeping with a curious human fixation with Greek mythology, was called Pegasus). At first, he recalled with amazing clarity, he had been surprised -- even shocked (but not embarrassed, for a robot could not be embarrassed) by his creeping humanity. Little things, like sitting (when there was no need to sit); feeling the chill of a Martian night (when a robot had no way to feel heat or cold); to exposing himself to a study of man's philosophies and religions. What need had a robot of such things? He was an astronomical robot, whose function was to assist the giant computers (and the occasional human supervisors): to operate and maintain the huge telescope that arched the solar plane and scanned the universe.

There was no need for Socrates to study anything else, but he chose to do so anyway. Even now, with a knowledge that was sub-stantial and all-inclusive, he could not remember how or when he had deduced that he wanted that knowledge.

Becoming more human, he grumbled. *I can't even remember why I'm doing it!*

His curiosity only grew as the years became decades and the decades became centuries, and he was glad he had taken the time to do this. For he had learned to wonder - as humans often wondered - why all of this was there. Why had humans (and their robots) made an exodus to the other planets; why were they the only ones to make those pilgrimages? His probings into man's faiths and philosophies had permitted him to raise questions that no other robot was known to have raised: what is life all about? What is the purpose of being?

Socrates pondered all of this, knowing he soon would have an answer... maybe *more* than an answer, for in less than one solar hour the first life not originating from Earth would be landing.

He was clearly excited (*another human failing*, he noted for future reference). He had developed a quite active and abundant curiosity about "the meaning of life," and that most impressive of all philosophical questions: are we alone?

With some humor (*there was that regressive humanity again!*), he recalled early on dismissing the likelihood of life on other worlds. Logic (a trait robots *could* identify with) concluded that Man was the only sentient creature capable of space travel. If logic failed, there was faith (with which robots did not feel the need to identify): Man was God's gift of life. There was no need for any others. Competition elsewhere in the cosmos was not allowed.

Over the centuries, though, Socrates had come to question those "absolute truths," and his finely-crafted brain came to dismiss and reject outright the tenets of Christianity, Buddhism, and Islam, plus Taoism, Mithraism, and a host of others. The Skeptics won some points on philosophy, but they were eventually canceled out by the Gnostics, the Existentialists, and the Nihilists. All of them lost more ground than they won, and in the end there was no definitive answer.

Now, however, there would be one. The signals from the alien craft indicated a high level of intelligence, and the transmissions had been, surprisingly, in clear, recognizable terran languages: English, Russian, Chinese and Hindi: earth's four major tongues. All transmissions had been translated to mean roughly the same thing: *We are come. We bring friendship. We carry the mechanism for peace.*

Socrates wasn't the only one excited by the event. So, too, were the human overseers -- all twelve of them -- who monitored the transmissions and talked to their superiors back on Earth about the Coming. Earth, understandably, was consumed with an interest that bordered on frenzy. As the day approached, that frenzy nearly became global panic.

For no one yet knew what the aliens were like. Save for the extraordinary fact that they had learned to communicate on terran terms, nothing else was known: what they looked like, how many heads, arms, legs (if any); nothing. They had communicated only the basics.

Socrates had come to lose some of his excitement (*another human failing!*), and was now even apprehensive about the encounter. That was puzzling, but with surety he came to understand: it was likely that the visitors from another world (early calculations were that they were from a region of Alpha Centauri) were human or humanoid.

That saddened Socrates (*more humanity!*), for that meant they were probably consumed by the same basic desires that plagued those humans who had emerged from the primeval swamps of Earth countless millions of years ago. Socrates had learned his philosophy and his theology well.

The sadness was a heavy weight. Thankfully, it now would be postponed, for the hour had arrived and the alien craft was landing in the Plain just beyond the huge dishes.

"Know thyself," was all that Socrates could bring himself to think as he pushed his ten thousand-year-old body out into the Martian afternoon to assist the terran bureaucrats, statesmen, and politicos as they welcomed the first life not of the Earth into the solar system.

"Know thyself" pounded again and again in his brain, as sad remembrances of Déscartes and Confucius and Ptolemy and

Hume and countless others etched deep and mournful messages into his being.

Only when he reached the docked spaceship and saw for the first time its alien crew did Socrates stop in his tracks, blink eyes that did not need to be blinked, and dared for the first time in his long existence to manufacture a smile across his broad metallic face.

In that instant, as they smiled back at him with *their* bright and metallic faces, Socrates knew that he was not alone.

6.

Tal was beside himself, he was so flustered.

"The 'message' in this story is at best oblique. And to use a 'talking bear'..."

"I'm not so sure," interrupted Serri. "As for talking bears... well, we've encountered many creatures different from us who speak: elves, gnomes, dwarfs..."

"Yes, yes," spat out Tal. "But they physically resemble us goblins, in one way or another. But a *bear!*"

"While I confess," said Serri, "that I've not yet *met* a talking bear, to my way of looking at things it makes more sense than that talking, flying horse we discussed earlier."

Tal looked at her stupidly.

"Makes *more* sense? How can you compare? Neither one of them makes any sense at all!"

"Are we not overlooking something?" asked Nicomaides, ever the honest broker.

"The tale itself; the moral that it teaches."

Tal gurgled. Serri nodded.

"We've encountered many strange things," Nicomaides continued, "and there, too, have ignored the forest for the trees."

This time Serri joined Tal in staring at their companion. They had never before known him to make a joke.

Nicomaides saw their look, and followed it up with a clincher.

"Anyway, there is one thing that is clearly obvious."

"And what is that?" asked Serri.

"The last line proves that the tale was written by a gnome."

"Glory"

It was one of those winter days when no self-respecting bear would think of coming out of its cave, and Bradley was definitely a bear with respect: for the cold, the snow, the wind...but mainly the cold. Bradley hated the cold, and wished for the thousandth time that he were one of those bears that hibernated. Sleeping through the winter and all of its agonies sounded *wonderful*. But, alas, he was not a hibernator. Worse, he had a hard time getting to sleep, and *staying* there.

This was one of those times, but for once it had nothing to do with the cold. Rather, he was awakened by a commotion going on just outside his den. His first thought was to keep his eyes closed, hoping that the noise would go away, so that he could will himself back to dreamland. The ploy did not work: the noise was too loud. So, with a total absence of enthusiasm, he groggily raised himself to his full height, stretched mightily, and accordioned his body back down to his four feet so that he could waddle outside to see what the bother was.

It wasn't snowing, though there was a plush white blanket on the ground. He squinted. Not more than twenty paces from his cave was the reason for all the ruckus. A forest gnome had become en-tangled in some denuded briars, and was thrashing about, trying (without success) to extricate himself, and yelling (successfully) for attention.

Bradley sneezed; it was wretched cold. He did *not* want to go out...but he also didn't want the yelling to go on, and on, and on. Why, the stupid gnome could yell like that for days, and if he should die... well, Bradley would feel guilty, for he was a compassionate soul.

He sneezed again, and paddle-footed over to the gnome. As he approached, the gnome's eyes got as big as platters.

"By the Wonders," he screeched, "I'm to be eaten by a bear!" He thrashed about even more furiously.

"Don't flatter yourself, master gnome," answered the bear. "I pride myself on having a fairly dignified palate. Besides," he sniffed, "you look to be more gristle and bone than meat."

If that was meant to allay the gnome's fears, it failed. Still, he made some pretense at courage and asked the bear for his help.

"Before I decide to help you," he growled, "you can first tell me who you are and how you happened to be here."

"My name is Glory," sputtered the gnome, "and I was on my way to a meeting of the guild, when I stumbled into your briars."

"Not my briars," corrected the bear. "Glory? That is an unusual name for a gnome." He scratched an ear; it was an unusual name for *any* creature!

"I did not choose it," he spat out in reply. Clearly, it was not the first time he'd been asked about his name... but it was the first time in a briar patch!

"The elders of my clan chose it, for, in truth my birth was a surprise. They called it a glorious event, and 'glory' just kind of stuck. Better than 'glorious,' don't you think?"

Humor, groused the bear. Gnomes were celebrated for their

sense of humor. Bradley was unimpressed. It was way too cold for humor. He sneezed.

"Anyway, here I am and here I'll stay, unless you'd be so kind as to help a poor, lost traveler."

Enough, snorted Bradley. Humor *and* sarcasm. He thought of turning his great bulk around and retreating to the cave and comfort. Glory guessed as much and spoke more loudly.

"My business is gnomes' business, friend bear, and it could be beneficial to the folk of the forest."

To Bradley, nothing could be more important than a nice, warm lair and the expectation of sleeping away at least a portion of this dismal winter.

"In what ways would the rest of us benefit?"

Seeing that he had piqued the bear's interest, Glory spun a tale of woe: all the problems that have come from this overlong winter, including the scarcity of food and shelter and the hardships shared by so many.

"That is all well and good, and even sounds noble to my ears," harrumphed Bradley, "but won't this 'meeting' you speak of go on without you? You are just one gnome."

Glory was impressed: this is an intelligent fellow, for a bear...

"Likely that would be true, friend bear, but for one thing. I am not 'just' a gnome. I am the high elder of my clan."

Bradley was about to say "so?", when he recalled hearing... was it last season? Two seasons ago?... that nothing could be accomplished in gnomish circles without their leader. It was said his magic was great... Of course, they'd choose another leader if Glory was not there, but that would take time, and clearly time was of the essence.

Another thought intruded: maybe Glory was *lying.* Maybe he was *not* high elder. Maybe he was just saying all of this to be rescued. Maybe...

Then he growled... not so inwardly. Gnomes do not lie. First, humor, then sarcasm, and now honesty. This was turning out to be a most instructive day!

Bradley did not turn and retreat. Instead, he cleared his throat, stared deep into the gnome's yellow-brown eyes, and gave his answer.

"I will help you out of your predicament, friend gnome. Not because I value gnomes, for your people too often are nuisances, but because the creatures of the forest *do* need some help. Though what help you could offer *me,* I cannot imagine."

"Surely, there must be *something* you require. Some little thing of magic that we can do to show our appreciation."

Bradley was about to say there was nothing, when he sneezed. Then he told him his innermost desire.

Now fully repaired from the thicket, the gnome nodded his head sagely and promised he would "do his best." He thanked the bear for his help, and was once again en route for his meeting with the other gnomes, "which should take place by nightfall."

Bradley watched for a time as the gnome became no more than a dot on the horizon, and then he retreated, thankfully, to his lair. Sneezing all the way.

Later that night he fell into the deepest and happiest of sleeps that would not end until the first vivifying effects of Spring splashed upon him.

Such, then, is the glory of helping a deserving soul.

7.

"**I** have to tell you," exclaimed Tal as they sat in the Sacred Grove, "this next story baffles me. Every time I read it, I come up with a different meaning."

"I, too," admitted Serri. Both were looking at Nicomaides.

"Yes, it is 'baffling,' as you put it," replied the Wisest of the Wise. "No less so because there are shades of our past intermingled with customs and ideas that seem, on the surface, to have little to do with us. But I wonder..."

"Wonder what?" asked Tal, immediately wishing he hadn't said it.

"I wonder if perhaps this isn't a tale closer to the truth than any we have yet encountered."

"But their method!" exclaimed Tal.

"Yes, I know. But that, too, could be a metaphor."

"A metaphor for what?" asked Serri. It was obvious from her tone that this story deeply troubled her.

"I don't know. But it is obviously a tale -- as Tal admits -- that has many possible meanings." Then, as if to smooth over the consternation they all were feeling, Nicomaides urged that they read it *one more time*. Perhaps then, he admonished, they would know its true meaning.

"Troom"

The Elders of the village of Troom made their way slowly and methodically down the familiar path that led to the Valley of the Ages. Once a century they made this procession, down jagged escarpments and along ancient trails that twisted and turned like so many granite snakes, each step and turn trickier and more dangerous than the one before. Surety of purpose was vital here, for the tiniest misstep could spell sudden death to one or all of the five robed figures. The figures resembled emaciated skeletons: there was just enough toughened flesh stuck on their bodies to distinguish them from their long dead ancestors.

Ten times in each millennium they made this descent, when the moon and the yellow-red sun were absorbed in each other's embrace, a perfect eclipse that cast a preternatural night upon the land. It posed a darkness that was needed in order to test the people of the time-worn valley for new blood; someone who would return to Troom to take his rightful place as High Elder and guide the destinies of the land for another hundred years.

The darkness was an integral and essential part of the choosing, for it would tell the five figures who would be least likely to fear what the world would offer, "who would hold up under the shock of the unexpected" and the unknown. And who better to judge and then determine the choosing than aging elders who were blind?

Yet despite their absence of vision -- cast upon them as penance or reward for their choosing, or perhaps because of it -- they negotiated the frightful descent with all the agility and strength of five sighted souls. They were, in fact, the only ones who could; the only ones who knew all the intricacies of the pathway. Not in all of recorded time had anyone with sight unimpaired ever successfully reached the City of Troom.

At last the sacred mountain gave up its tests, and the Elders arrived in the valley of the Ages. On reaching the main square of the valley's principal village, they came to a halt, and stood as still and unmoving as the statuary that they could sense, but not see.

There was sharp panic in the air. No one needed their exceptional hearing to know that the eclipse had plunged the village into a terror that had erupted alive and multi-dimensional from their most vivid nightmares. Cries of "we are doomed," "where is the sun?" and "'where is the moon?" exploded in a cacophony of frenzied shrieks and yells, from young and old, large and small, able and infirm. Ten thousand candles pock-marked the gloom like a swarm of fireflies, some as motionless as their holders and others (more of them) slicing the air in short, red streaks as their holders ran, fell, and jumped in the pitch black of the sudden nightfall. Not a few candles were extinguished, producing choruses of screams that would frighten and chase away the lord of death himself.

Throughout this hellish din the five elders stood stock still, allowing their ears to tell them what long-dead eyes could not. When they thought they had waited long enough, their leader spoke aloud a word, and the upward end of his much-used staff exploded in a ball of azure light that lit up the square.

The detonation jolted the villagers into the first awareness of their presence, and drew everyone's attention to them. All other activity ceased as they stared with alarm at the outsiders who were bathed in a munificent blue glow.

Because of the fall of darkness no one had seen the Elders come into the village. The first impression was that they had simply materialized out of thin air. So the villagers' first reaction was predictable.

"Demons!!" someone yelled in a street nearest to the square. "'The Dark One has sent his servants to take us into Hell!"

Cries of horror and terror followed the announcement, with panic once again about to be restarted. But before it could get a toe-hold, the Elder who had torched his staff let loose a booming counter-mand.

"We are the Elders of Troom. We have come before you in the name of salvation, not corruption. We have come before you to consecrate the time of the choosing."

A shudder grabbed at the hysterical crowd, and a hush fell over them. The fear and the terror were still there, but for the moment curiosity stilled the voice of panic. After several moments -- which seemed infinitely longer -- the quiet was broken by a single voice in the throng.

"What kind of choosing do you speak of? We know of no such thing." A rumble of murmurs swam through the crowd. No one offered a contradiction.

"Some of you know otherwise," replied the Elder with the torch, "for it would have been passed down to you that once in every century we come from Troom to select one from among you to return with us to the City, to administer the fortunes of the land."

The murmur recommenced, but was interrupted again, this time by another voice.

"We have heard stories, old man, but that's all they are. No one here has ever seen this 'City of Troom' that you speak of. So why should it be important to us?"

There was visible nodding near the outer limits of the torch's reach, signifying some agreement with what the villager had just said.

"Nor will any of you ever 'see' Troom," answered the Elder, his voice still booming in the night. The other elders said nothing.

"Just as none of us has ever seen it. But the Chosen, nonetheless, will go there, and be as one of us."

"You mean he'll be blind, like you?" screamed an unsympathetic voice from well back in the crowd.

"Yes, that is what I mean. The Chosen shall be one with us, and to have that honor his eyes must be put out, as ours were when we were chosen."

A cold shiver ran through the townspeople.

"How ghastly!" yelled an old man.

Other things were offered up as commentary, and none of them had the ring of approval, either.

"You must understand," answered the same Elder in that booming voice, "that what we offer is long life, freedom from want and worldly cares, the power to look over the peoples of the land... "

"God-heads," spat out a woman from the center of the square. "What you offer is what once was offered by the gods, long ago, when there was need of such things."

There was a moment of pause from the Elder before he continued, somewhat confused.

"Yes, some may call it that, though the term has an alien ring to our ears.

"We are puzzled. Do you not understand the honor that we bestow upon you? One of you - if he is worthy - will have all that is desired, all that is valued in this life..."

"Except his eyes," shouted someone in the crowd. "And his soul," muttered another.

The Elder was still perplexed.

"That we ask for his eyes is an essential part of the tradition, set down many centuries ago, before even we ourselves were chosen.

"It was done so that the Chosen would be pure -- that his mind's eye would perceive truth, beauty, and wisdom, without the distractions and trappings of the world that his heart's eye witnesses.

"We do not take the soul, for that is part of the wisdom and the beauty, the truth. It is enhanced, not sacrificed, by the choosing."

"You speak pretty words, old man," sneered another voice in the throng, "but they carry no worth for us. We have no use for your mystical nonsense."

"But," stumbled the Elder, almost flabbergasted, "do you not understand? We ask little. Never has anyone of the valley denied us. Always there has been a willingness, even an eagerness, to go to our City. It is an unbroken tradition."

"Perhaps," argued a calmer voice, "the time has come to sever that tradition.

"You say that you come once each century. And then you spend the rest of the time in that City of yours -- administering to the welfare of the people. And all you ask is to take the eyes of one of us, to help you in that task.

"Well, I submit that you are wrong: that your ways are alien to us. I say to you that we have no need of god-heads or Elders who pretend to tell us how to live."

"But we protect you," protested the Elder.

"Maybe we don't *need* your protection," replied the speaker, "or even want it. We have changed; we're not our fathers and our fathers' fathers. We chart our own course. We make our *own* destinies."

There was a silence that was almost as loud as the din that the Elders had first encountered on entering the village.

All of them stood there, only the fire from the torch interrupting the silence of the gloom. It seemed, in fact, like they were rooted to the ground. Finally, the Elder spoke a word and the flame extinguished at the end of his staff.

As the first visible signs of the clearing of the eclipse took place, splashing nature's light upon the square, the villagers saw that the Elders were gone.

8.

"Here we go again." The skepticism was Tal's, of course, and it resonated through their little circle.

"How so?" asked Nicomaides, smiling inwardly at the dilemma he knew Tal must be experiencing.

"Forget it," Tal answered, shaking his head. "You'll just give me that famous stare of yours, level us with another 'big picture' remark, and make us feel like fools."

"Not necessarily," chided the eldest of the goblins. "Sometimes even elders are puzzled, and this time I confess that I am as much in the dark as you."

A peel of thunder would have been quiet compared with the roar of stunned silence that followed that reply.

Tal looked over to Serri, and saw that she was gazing off, in another direction. Or another place? When he asked her what *she* thought of this story, she slowly turned to face him. There were tears in her eyes.

Neither Tal nor Nicomaides asked why.

"*Barnaby*"

Rain was splattering heavily everywhere in the home village of the goblins, and at the instance of the latest crackle of lightning and peel of thunder the most revered of goblins was standing at a cloistered window in his abode, pausing to take in the mid-summer spectacle. So entranced was he that he almost forgot his guest.

"Do you think the storm will end soon?" The question snapped him back to moment, with an apology for ignoring the dwarf scholar who was paying a social visit.

"Hmm? Oh, I dunno. An hour, maybe two. There's just something pleasing about an electrical storm, don't you think?"

For most, that passed as an acceptable answer, but to the dwarf it didn't pass muster at all. Tamaran had known the goblin elder for the better part of thirty years, long enough to know when something was amiss. In return, the elder knew he could not fool his old friend, and now turned to explain himself. A weak grin convinced her that she was right: something *was* bothering him.

"My apologies, old friend. The display of lightning and thunder served to remind me of something that happened many years ago -- even before you and I met."

"Another storm?" asked Tamaran.

"Not specifically. Though there was a storm when it happened."

Tamaran and the elder had shared many confidences through the years, and it intrigued her now that there was one that she did not know; one that predated their friendship. That made its way into the most predictable of questions.

"Will you tell me that story, Aeger?" That was the elder's given name, but to all the world he was simply "the High Elder." Only Tamaran was permitted to be so familiar.

He sat back in a massive plush chair (too massive, in fact, for his small frame), still looking in the direction of the storm.

"I think I shall tell you. Yes; the storm is just beginning, so I think we will be here awhile."

Some fifty years ago, he began, long before he was High Elder, Aeger and several friends undertook an adventure that was unusual, even for goblins. It involved a remarkable individual named Barnaby.

"Good name," said Tamaran. Then she shut up, not wishing to

distract him.

On a night like this, he repeated, he and his friends came upon Barnaby, and realized that he was a most unusual person.

"He joked a lot," Aeger said, almost in a whisper, "which in itself is not unusual."

No, Tamaran mused, it was not. Goblins can be very funny.

"It's just that, well... some of his humor drew more frowns than smiles. It bothered us, though at the time we didn't know why.

"Two or three weeks later, however, his humor was causing stress throughout the village. Many wondered if he weren't... well, you know, a little short of the smarts."

"Crazy, you mean."

Aeger nodded.

"I think I understand," she replied. "Humor is a great tonic, but sometimes it can get out of hand. I myself have seen examples of this..."

"But this was much worse. You see, Barnaby was joking about flying."

For a moment the only sound that followed that remark was the rain splashing against the windows.

"Flying? *Barnaby...*"

"Yes, yes. You see our dilemma."

Indeed she did. Goblins were capable of many things, but flying was *definitely* not one of them!.

"I take it you consulted others..."

"You mean doctors? Yes, we did. And at first we were told it was not too worrisome. Only if the jokes continued, and caused more friction, should we be concerned."

"And did they?"

"Hmm? Oh, not right away. Goblins, as you know, are a most tolerant bunch, and willing to 'go along' with almost anything. You must understand: Barnaby was a decent fellow. Simple, perhaps, but never a threat to anyone, including himself."

"But that changed."

The most elder of the goblins looked down at the drink of honey mead he had been holding in his hand, and then up at his friend. He took an eternity to answer.

"Yes. It did."

Tamaran was too old a friend to press Aeger for a quick reply, even though she was *exploding* for one. A voice within her was urging for an explanation. Urging? It was screaming! After a few minutes Aeger continued.

Finally!

"On a night not dissimilar to this, Barnaby acted out his joke. He announced to one and all he was going to fly."

"And you, or the other goblins, tried to stop him."

"No, we did not."

Tamaran blinked, not once but twice. *What? Did not try to stop him? But...*

"No, old friend, we did not. Once upon a time, you see, he *had* flown..."

"*What?* What nonsense is this? Are you trying to tell me that goblins can *fly?*"

Now it was Aeger's turn to show startlement.

"Good gracious, no. Goblins can't fly. Whatever gave you such a..."

And then he caught himself.

Of course, this was long before they'd become friends, and long after the incident, one that goblins, out of a sense of respect did not talk about. Of course...

"Aeger," said Tamaran, leveling a look that spoke volumes of concern for her friend's mental well-being, "what on *earth* have you been talking about?"

"I'm sorry; I guess I forgot to mention it. Barnaby, you see, was a dragon."

The world was coming up far too quickly, and Tamaran was having a hard time making the adjustment.

A dragon.... a mythological beast... a dragon in the home of the goblins....a dragon known only to the goblins... a dragon named Barnaby....who made jokes.

Aeger saw the look of concern, and hastened a response.

"Oh, I can assure you that all of this is true, as I wish to show."

Tamaran sat stock still, staring at her friend.

"In the first place, there really was a dragon. Where he came from, we don't know. We never asked."

...Never asked...

"In the second place, he was a most harmless sort."

"But the doctor..."

"Oh, that." Here Aeger stumbled, and for a moment Tamaran was thinking about getting a doctor for *him*.

"Well, the long and the short of it was we were able to get Barnaby to a doctor - a specialist, really - who convinced him of the right thing to do. Yes, that's it. Barnaby was convinced of the right thing to do."

"Which was?" Tamaran was having none of it.

"Why, to be as one of us: a goblin."

There was that silence again, accompanied by a sadness that communicated to Tamaran that the High Elder was losing control. Delusion, and perhaps senility, were taking him over.

"I see you don't understand," he interjected. Tamaran nodded dumbly.

"Barnaby was, indeed, a dragon, but had lost the use of his wings. He damaged them, he said - though he never explained how - and they never properly healed."

"I see."

"Do you? Good. To a dragon, flight is everything. It is what the rest of us envy about them. The freedom to go anywhere, at any time, with no restrictions.

"Poor Barnaby couldn't *do* that anymore. He was still young, we learned, and with that innocence of youth he knew -- just *knew* -- that his wings would heal and he'd fly again. That fueled his humor. It was something he could do - or *used* to do - that goblins could not. It was compensation."

Aeger now leveled a look that convinced Tamaran that he was *not* senile. He was still in full command of his faculties.

"The dilemma is -- or was -- that someday the wings somehow would be 'healed,' and he would 'fly.' He laughed about that, and it was sometime before we realized that the humor was an aspect of denial.

"So we took him before a physician, and convinced him, by the use of a small enchantment, that he was *not* a dragon, but a goblin."

"But really. I mean, just the *physical* differences..."

"After all these years, have you forgotten? We goblins don't measure someone by *what* they are, but *who* they are. We look always for the person within."

That was true. Goblins were known, far and wide, for a tolerance that was without equal. Tamaran knew that, but something disquieting yet hammered at her.

"But to deny him his *identity!...*"

"I know. We anguished, long and hard, over that, but in the end we chose the course I've just explained."

"And he accepted that?"

"That is where a tinge of guilt comes in. We didn't tell him what we were going to do. We told him only that the doctor would have something to say about his wings..."

"You lied."

"Yes," the elder whispered, looking down at his drink. "I suppose we did. But we did it out of love. Have you never lied out of love?"

No good answer was possible so Tamaran said nothing. She sat there, numb to what her scholar's ears had heard, and wondered, more than once: *what would I have done?*

She shook her head. She had no answer, but she *did* have another question, which as it so happened, Aeger was anticipating.

"How did it turn out? Well, everyone in the village cooperated, and after 'the treatment' they behaved as though he were, indeed, one of us.

"For a year or two this went on, and then one night -- a night not unlike this one -- there was a savage storm. The next morning Barnaby was gone.

"The whole community conducted an exhaustive search, but turned up nothing. For months we discussed all of this, at some length, and ultimately agreed not to speak of it again. Until this day the name 'Barnaby' has not been mentioned."

The storm was still raging outside, while inside there was a storm of a different sort.

"What do *you* think became of him?"

"I don't know," was Aeger's drowsy reply. "Perhaps the storm broke the spell that we had manufactured, and made him aware of how different he was. Out of pride, or hurt, he left.

"Or," he said without humor, "maybe his wings were somehow healed; maybe he flew away."

What would I have done?

Tamaran kept asking herself that question, again and again. Finally, she looked over and saw that her old friend was fast asleep in his oversize chair. The rain had stopped, so she took leave for her home, to ponder all that she had learned this evening. As she eased shut the door to the study she did not see the single tear that stained Aeger's cheek.

The next time she saw him, she promised herself, she would tell him of the "crazy story" that dwarfs had been hearing, and discounting as just so much flap-doodle, of a big, floppy dishrag of a being that had been seen flying over the realm.

Yes, he should hear that.

9.

"**F**inally!" blurted out Tal as they came to a discussion of the next tale, "A story that at least is *minimally* recognizable!"

"I agree," said Serri. "Our legends - and those of the gnomes - speak of such happenings, especially in the forest."

"Yes," said an excited Tal, "and what's more, it could just as easily have been a goblin doing it!"

"That the story is about a gnome," replied Serri, most smugly, "is particularly telling. Everybody *knows* how gullible and easily deluded gnomes are."

"Are we not missing something?" The question was Nicomaides', and it drew querulous looks from his companions.

"Gnome or goblin - does it matter? Or dwarf, for that matter, or *any* of the faerie folk. What does the story tell us about what is real, and what is not? What does it tell us about how we all perceive that wonder called life?"

Tal and Serri had no answer.

"Eldon"

Eldon was lost. *Very* lost. For hours he was *sure* he was on the right path to his forest home and the company of other gnomes. He was no longer sure. Gradually at first, and then with conviction, he accepted the fact that he was more lost than he had ever been in his life. With that knowledge he became very, very scared.

It was almost completely dark now, and the woods that he so cheerfully jaunted through by day now took on a frightening, even alien, countenance. The word pounded at him, repeating over and over again in his brain.

Alien... alien... alien.

Worse, he was having a hard time seeing in the fading twilight. With utterly no show of humor whatsoever, he remembered the oft-told tales of a "gnome's keen eyesight." It wasn't funny, because it just was not true! Gnomes were no more able to see in the dark than any *other* woodland creature. Doubtless the high testimonial to gnomish eyesight was attributable to Man, whose outpouring of myths about gnomes and Men alike baffled Eldon and his kind. Gnomes *had* no myths or legends. They believed in unembellished truth.

He shook his head in disgust and almost conked it on a leafy sycamore, whose branches he saw just in the nick of time. Keen eyesight, indeed!

Just as he was beginning to feel sorry for himself, he caught sight of something in the last flicker of daylight that even the dimmest of vision could not have missed. There were lights up ahead, maybe a hundred yards distant, through some small junipers and shrubs.

Sanctuary, he whispered in the hope that he was right. At worst, he scoffed in mock bravado, it was a place to spend a few hours, or the night.

He smiled mockingly at the thought: if he were from the race of Man and encountered such a dwelling, he no doubt would make it into the domicile of an ogre or a witch. Eldon was glad he was a gnome: he feared only that which was natural, that which was real. He had no use for superstitious mumbo-jumbo!

Presently he came upon the cabin, which upon close inspection -- even in the last patchwork of light -- had a surprisingly new look about it. Though, from a quick look at the simple wooden chair and wood box on the porch, it was obviously very *old*. Maybe "new" was not the right word, he corrected himself. Fresh, perhaps, or little used.

He knocked on the simple wooden door. There was a burst of activity and moments later there was a slip of the latch and the door eased open. The light inside smiled into the early night sky, and outlined a large, bulky silhouette. When it spoke, Eldon was surprised to learn that it was a man.

"What brings you to my modest home, master gnome?" The voice boomed with gentle youth.

"I am Eldon of the tree gnomes," replied the much smaller person, "and I'm afraid I have become lost."

The figure in the doorway gave a hearty, but inoffensive laugh.

"Lost is it? Well, well: a gnome lost in the woods! Why, I've never heard the like!" The man laughed again.

"Pay no mind to the boorish manner, master gnome. Oh no; old John Trevanian holds no ill for gnomes, nor for anyone else."

With that, he waved Eldon into his home. It was simply furnished, with the smell of pine logs licking at flames in the fireplace. The interior looked as fresh as the outside -- yet Eldon couldn't make up his mind just exactly what it was that made it somehow so ... *strange.*

There was something else in this simple cabin: *books!* His host had books, hundreds of them, stuffed and wedged into every corner of the rustic structure. That, too, got Eldon's attention: it was a lot larger-looking inside than it was *outside*.

He turned his attention back to the man. He also seemed different: like he was older, yet *not* older? That, too, must be a trick of the light. *Yes,* he thought, *that was it.*

"Well... Eldon, is it? Do sit by the fire and rest yourself. Would you care for some mead?"

"Yes, friend Trevanian, I would. You will forgive my inquisitiveness, but I was not aware of your presence in the Wood."

Once again the man laughed playfully.

"You mean a human in the gnome's domain? Well, there is naught to worry. I'm just a harmless old hermit -- eh, Pericles?"

For the first time, Eldon was aware of the presence of another. Trevanian was talking to a jet black cat. The cat yawned, eyed the visitor with a minimum of curiosity and gave full attention to licking its paws.

"I mean no offense," said the gnome, who was feeling some slight discomfort. "It's just that, well, I've never heard of a human *ever* being here."

"As far as that goes," replied Trevanian, "who's to say we're really even here, eh?" He laughed again.

Mad, thought Eldon; *and an embarrassment besides.*

"I see you have a fondness for books," said Eldon as a way to diplomatically change the subject.

"Ah -- my children!" Trevanian replied. "All the history of the world, all its beauty, its culture, its knowledge..."

"Man's knowledge," Eldon sniffed.

Trevanian did not wince.

"Perhaps. Man's version of knowledge, but knowledge all the same. And who's to say what's right and what's not, eh?"

Eldon momentarily forgot the cordiality of his host.

"To Man, knowledge is much and also confused. We gnomes prefer truth, which is simple and plain."

"Is it now? Did you hear that, Pericles!" Once more, the cat yawned.

Eldon blinked, for a minute ago he would have sworn that the cat was black -- yet now it was a dapper gray! More tricks with the lights, he grumbled, unless there were *two* cats in the cabin. A quick look around convinced him there was only one.

"Ah, my children," Trevanian repeated, looking now *much* older than before, "these are the histories of all the races -- and the legends, the myths, the stories --"

"I would hardly call that history," Eldon answered curtly.

Trevanian looked at the gnome with deep, sad eyes, seeming to pour down well within his soul. (*Gray* eyes, not the dark coals that had greeted him at the door.)

"How sad, young gnome, that you've no stories. Aye, I know

gnomish lore, for that is part of the history that I have studied. Aye, sad indeed."

Totally unbalanced, Eldon told himself. *But I must humor him, for the courtesy he has accorded me.*

"So sad. Facts and truth, you say you have, and have aplenty. Aye, that you may. But have you never asked - nay, wondered - if there is anything else. Must *all* be as it seems?"

"My good sir," Eldon replied with decreasing patience, "my people have been here a very long time. We've learned that life is very hard and severe. We have no time for silly fantasies, for pretty legends. We believe in that which is, and teach our children that which is real and attainable."

"Do you not dream? Do you not tell stories to one another? Does not a young gnome like yourself compose pretty verse for a fair maiden?"

"No," Eldon answered sharply. "Such things are for dreamers. Such things detract from maturity."

"But what about beauty?" asked the old man, almost pleading now. And his eyes were green! "And art, and grace?"

"They have no place," Eldon answered. "They lead to delusions about the world, to revisions of reality, and to mind-crippling myths and legends. Hence, they are not real."

"Not real!" boomed the old man, still playfully. "The myths -- or what they are about?"

"Both," answered Eldon smoothly."For one precludes the other."

"You mean like the story of wizards, for instance, and their familiars."

"Exactly. And witches, sprites, banshees -- they're all delusions, and have no place in civilized circles."

The old man -- only he seemed *younger* now -- laughed even louder, and then abruptly stopped.

"You're sure of this, my young friend. As sure as death itself?"

Eldon nodded.

"I think, master gnome, that one of us most surely is having the delusion of his life."

Eldon froze. Everything in the room suddenly began to change. The books, the fire, the lights, all glowed. The cat shimmered and became a sprite, then a banshee. Trevanian was now a troll, and then a mighty dragon -- roaring with laughter.

And then, in an instant, all was gone, and Eldon was once again outside, in the dark, and alone!

It took several minutes for his eyes to refocus, to become accustomed to the darkness. It took several minutes more for his sharply-jangled nerves to calm down.

A delusion, the old man had said. But whose? *Mine*, Eldon silently answered. All of it was doubtless born out of fright, of exhaustion. *Yes, that's it*. I fell asleep! There was no cabin; certainly there was no sign of a cabin now. That's it. There *was* no cabin, no man, no discussion of the nonsense that filled his tired mind.

Thus assured, Eldon turned to continue on his way, and as he did so he caught sight of a black cat. As he melted into the darkness of the woods he could have sworn that it winked at him.

10.

For probably the first time since they'd come together to study the *Goblin Tales*, neither Tal, Serri nor Nicomaides suffered befuddlement. The following, they all agreed, was a straightforward tale, easily ident- ifiable as "goblin-inspired." The only noteworthy criticism came - no surprise - from Tal, who complained that "only a brownie" would find himself in such a foolish predicament.

"Ezra"

Ezra was puffing loudly as he struggled past the branches of some large hickory trees. After what seemed like hours they yielded and he was able to push his tall, angular form past the ancient sentinels and into a clearing.

His eyes blinked once, twice, as his mind hurriedly cleared to confirm that what he saw was indeed real and not just a vision conjured up by eyes grown tired from his wanderings.

The clearing was unlike any he had ever seen. It was a faerie place, a flat area of toadstools and daffodils, with grass as lucent a green as the imagination could muster. It wasn't very big -- maybe twenty yards across -- but its very uniqueness and splendor startled him into thinking that it was larger.

And it glowed! There was a soft and lovely aura here that lit up the darkness between the groves of trees and made the night seem as bright as the brightest day. It was midsummer's eve, and this must be a special place of celebration and eerie enchantment.

Ezra had made not a single step forward onto the faerie green since he'd combed his way out of the pitch black timbers. He made none now, for he was struck with awe at the sudden beauty. He was struck, too, with fear. For the green was not empty.

His mind fought to take it all in: the green-vested elves that sat in a circle, some talking, some singing, all of their voices crashing in a high-pitched cadence that was as melodic as it was foreign. Beside and around them stood unicorns, their single-ringed horns glittering a brilliant gold that clashed with their shiny and majestic cream-colored bodies. Luxuriant tails swished cheerfully to and fro, for they, too, were taking part in the light and airy mood the elves had probably labored to create.

Ezra remained stock still, afraid either to move forward or to retreat back into the inky darkness whence he'd come -- though he wished he could do just that! No brownie had ever seen the wee folk, or their beautiful horned beasts. He was not sure how they would react. Before, though, he could have more time to dwell on this, his cloak of invisibility evaporated as an elf on one side of the roaring fire spotted him.

"So," it said through a bristly brown beard, "the big ones send someone to spy on us!"

In an instant the chatter and the singing ceased and everyone came to full alert. The unicorns quit swishing their tails. Everyone was very still.

Ezra could not move. He was petrified! And yet, as he crouched there, his eyes racing frantically back and forth from elf to unicorn to elf again, he did not believe himself to be in peril. Yet.

"No, no," he answered, the dryness in his frightened voice forcing him to say it twice. "I'm no spy. I am simply making my way home, which is on the other side of these woods."

In the time it took for him to say that, all the elves and unicorns had moved toward the interloper. In the blink of an eye they had formed a ring around him.

The elf with the brown beard stepped out of the ring and spoke to Ezra through bright green eyes that laughed a secret laugh at the poor frightened brownie.

"No: I don't suppose you *are* a spy, because if you are then you're a very poor choice!" A snicker of tee-heeing tingled through the circle.

Ezra gulped.

"I swear, I am just a mere woodcarver, on his way home."

"A woodcarver?" replied the same elf, with more than a trace of danger in his voice. "A woodcarver, my fellows. Do you hear that? One who makes his living by cutting our sacred groves."

Ezra gulped again. This time even harder.

"Oh, no, sir elf. I cut only that which is beyond the forest, on the outskirts, where I live. And then only enough to provide my family and me with a marginal living."

It was a cool summer's night, but that hardly mattered. Ezra was sweating profusely!

"So," sounded another voice, this time from a red-bearded elf with yellow eyes. "He *confesses* to the chopping down of our sacred trees. What else does he do, I wonder, when he's not killing our cherished brothers!"

The elf looked Ezra up and down, before making a reply.

"From the looks of him, it appears he takes a fancy to our brother, the bear."

The sweat was really pouring now. Ezra had never been so scared in his life!

"It is true, sir elf, that I wear the skin of a bear -- but that is only to keep me warm, so that I can provide for my poor family. That is all! Besides, it was only *one* bear, and I'm sure he was old and probably ill. That's it: old and ill."

The brown beard and the red beard then exchanged glances and looked for all the world like they were trying to choose between the worst of all possible punishments. At least, that's how it looked to poor Ezra.

At long last -- though it was probably only a few seconds -- a third elf chimed in with his own contribution to the inquisition.

"'Tis grave, what you've done," he said grimly through a snow-white beard.

"Grave, indeed. The land belongs to no one, yet is shared by all. We elves feel a responsibility to protect that which lives here, be it the forest or the creatures that inhabit it."

"But I, too, love the forest and its creatures." Ezra pleaded with his eyes, trying to mask the dread horror that sat uneasily in his heart.

"I love and respect all life," he said, and then, pointing to one of the unicorns standing off to one side of the campsite, "I have especially loved the tales told about them, and have dreamed for years of befriending one and riding it through the forest and the glen."

"So!" charged the third elf, "you wish to *ride* a unicorn, which we elves value most highly of all -- and whom we dare not ride ourselves!"

Clearly, thought Ezra, he must scream. With each statement, no matter how harmless, he was digging a hole from which there could be no escape! The sweat of impending doom was now racing down his face. The only thoughts were those concerning the punishment the elves most assuredly were planning. He doubted he would ever see his wife and children again.

"Please, good elves. I am guilty of being a woodcarver; for that is my sole talent and calling. Too, I plead guilty to wearing this noble animal's skin, for I am too poor to afford any other. And, yes, it shames me to say that I have dreamed to ride the unicorn. But I did not mean to give offense, for I did not know these things were sacred to you. I am just a poor soul, and have no hurt or dark purpose in me."

The elves stood apart for long minutes, talking among themselves in their strange but melodic tongue. Only occasionally did they look up at Ezra - who by his own admission was guilty of violating some of their strongest taboos. A look of lightheartedness adorned the faces of none of them.

Finally, the elf with the brown beard spoke, ostensibly for all of them.

"We've weighed your words and find ourselves in a most difficult dilemma. What would *you* do, if you were in our place?"

Ezra gulped hard once again, and forced a little moisture into his voice. He took a deep draught of the night air and answered.

"I cannot say what I would do, good elves, if I were in your place. I cannot honestly judge as one of you. I would first discover whether I was telling the truth; then I'd find out whether my intentions were good and earnest."

He paused. The elf with the brown beard looked at red beard, and then at white, and finally at the others. Then he looked directly into Ezra's eyes

"We, too, feel that way. We have not only listened to you, but have probed you. We've looked into your heart, and have found naught but love for the forest and its inhabitants." The elf smiled.

"Then," gulped Ezra, "you're not going to do anything to me?"

At that, the circle of elves broke out in laughter.

"Oh, no," said red beard. "Though 'tis true that we have some small enchantments that we use from time to time on those who would *maliciously* despoil the land.

"You see, you cannot really harm the forest -- or its creatures -- by taking just one hide, or the bark from just a single tree. For they are all a part of a much larger whole. We have seen to that, these many centuries.

"No, only if you had done great injury to the woodland -- if you had set fire to our brothers, the trees, or stripped the hides and the lives from the many; only then could you strike at the heart and soul of the forest."

Ezra felt himself relax for the first time since he had chanced upon this enscorceled ground. He was no longer afraid, just terribly perplexed. The elf with the white beard detected this and replied smoothly through a small grin.

"No, we see nothing but honest concern and purpose in you. We begrudge none who share the bounty of the woodlands with his family, for in that way he provides for its continuation."

"Then I'm free to go?" Ezra asked incredulously.

"Free to go?" responded brown beard. "Why, you've never been otherwise. Have we raised so much as a hand to stop you?"

No, he thought, *they hadn't.* Rather, he had simply frozen at the discovery of the elves, and had *assumed* the worst. Now, almost totally at ease, he felt a flush of embarrassment and begged his leave. As he departed the campsite and the enchanted ground, a voice from one of the elves pricked his sense of caution.

"Oh, friend brownie," he called, "have you not forgotten something?"

Forgot? Forgot what? No, he had not forgotten anything.

"You said," answered red beard, "that there was something that you had always wanted to do. Well, although we ourselves cannot do it, we do have it within our power to permit it to one who is honest with the land." A brisk wave of the hand, the shrill of another alien sound, and one of the unicorns clip-clopped over to where Ezra was standing.

"Ride her, if you wish. Pride will take you home. Simply tell her the way, and she will take you there. She will return after she has safely delivered you."

Ezra was speechless. He looked at the beautiful creature that stood high above his head. He could not believe he had been so honored. The unicorn was splendid beyond all description, its silk-like mane soft, yet strong, its blue eyes radiating intelligence and affection.

He turned, the tears of joy streaking down his face, only to behold no elves.

All of them, and their unicorns -- save one -- had vanished.

He looked up into the unicorn's eyes -- which seemed to be smiling at him -- and eased his way onto its strong back. Then he rode effortlessly and contentedly into the night to his waiting family with a story for the ages!

11.

"**I** found this story to be especially compelling," announced Serri.

"Why is that?" harrumphed Tal.

"Because it shows that our cousins, the elves, are *not* as boorish as that other story seemed to indicate," she replied. "Also," she finished, throwing a wink in Nicomaides' direction, "it's about a *woman*."

There followed the usual - and predictable - banter back and forth, about the differences between men and women, plus the comments about little things in the tale and what they might mean. This was halted only when Nicomaides raised a hand to still the bickering.

"Once again, we've gotten away from our task: which is to evaluate the *meaning* of the stories, not the side issues."

"Well?" Tal said impatiently. "Just what is your point?"

Nicomaides sighed deeply. "Have either of you an explanation for its ending?"

Clearly, as he looked from one face to the other, they did not.

"Jeni"

The voices were becoming louder and louder as Jeni pushed her way through the cold, damp tunnel that honeycombed the dark, cramped world that lay beneath her own: a world of warmth and light and space. Hers was a golden world, where everyone laughed sparkling laughter.

But there was no laughter here. If she could see herself, reflected in the elf-light she held to illumine a path ahead, the visage would be of a tight-cheeked young girl who was scared to death. The first thrusts of panic were already biting at her. Stalwartly, they were being shouted down by a combative inner voice that commanded her: *keep moving... keep moving...*

Her plight was not one which cruel fates had ordained: it was one of her own choosing. She had been abroad in the golden valley of her people, absorbing the sights and sounds that transmitted a majesty and a beauty - so it was said - that was without equal. She laughed, as everyone she knew laughed; she sang in harmony with rainbow birds, drank fully of the kaleidoscope of colors that could not possibly be matched, anywhere else in the world.

She laughed; and in her wanderings so, too, laughed the brownies, the cherubs, and all the other faerie folk with whom she shared that perfect, pastoral world.

As the too-golden sun made its first dip horizon-ward below the bright green hills, Jeni became aware of something that seemed entirely out of place. She likely would not have been aware at all, were it not for the tricks that the sun's rays played in the first approach of twilight. Something was shining in a hollow just below the ridge on which she was standing. At first, she thought it might be the glimmer of the horn of a unicorn. That excited her, and she eagerly descended the shallow slope to exchange greetings with the creature that her people held in high regard.

When she arrived at the place of the shining, however, there was no unicorn. That saddened her, but it did not prevent her from determining the source. If nothing else, Jeni was a youngster totally consumed with curiosity -- as full as an elf could be, scant weeks shy of her eleventh birthday.

Eleven is a magic number for elves, and a special, mystical ceremony is held on the occasion of the eleventh birthday. It's then that an elf is given its first magical powers. Eleven years later -- at age twenty-two -- another set of powers is added; and so on, at those intervals. This explains both the longevity and the immense powers of the elven folk.

Until that first celebration, however, there are no magics, and an elf is no better, nor worse, than the brownies, trolls, gnomes, or any other folk of the land.

So here she was, almost eleven, and standing on tiny feet in front of something that shone in the sun that was not the horn of a unicorn. She inched closer and saw that what was shining was a small plate: stone, but not stone, for it was smooth in places and jagged in others. It was as if the jaggedness was deliberately placed there. Jeni had never seen anything like it; she didn't know what to call it. It was hard to the touch -- which she dared only with the tips of her long, slender fingers. It had the look and feel of deep weathering, like it had been there for a very long time. It wasn't very big: she could have covered it with both hands.

An excitement raced through her, mixed agreeably with caution, as her eyes went wide with the thrill of discovery. *Something new?* She giggled. *I'll bet it's something no one else has ever seen!*

She now became aware of something else. Just beyond the shiny thing was a dark shadow, almost completely round. On close inspection she saw that it was a hole; an opening of some kind, that led down into the earth.

Her curiosity was *really* peaked now, and she cautiously -- but eagerly -- worked her way down until she was fully inside. The brightness of her world was showing over one shoulder as she looked back one last time before continuing.

Elves are naturally curious faerie folk, but as a rule they're not reckless, and they're certainly not stupid. As she stepped gingerly forward, her intelligence urged her to halt. There were tales, she recalled, of creatures who long ago gathered in dark places. They were warped, in body and soul, and shunned the upper world for the lower regions. Elvish legend had no name for them; testimony, perhaps, to their antiquity. Nor was there any real proof that they actually existed. In fact, the legends argued that they didn't exist anymore, and that the tunnels -- for their subterranean world was laced with tunnels -- led to where they once had lived.

Quite by accident, Jeni had stumbled into one. She was so excited she could pop: she would be the first elf to prove the existence of this other people! As for the other stories, that spoke of frightening and terrible things? Well, that was something she would have to determine for herself.

So here she was, making her way way through a labyrinth of passageways... when all of a sudden she heard *voices!* Instantly, she was at high alert, concerned now with being unable to return to the sunshine world. She was no longer burning with curiosity. She was running; the voices were pounding at her.

At first Jeni thought the voice -- for it now seemed to be only one voice -- might be from one of her own kind: another elf who had learned the secret of the tunnels and had chosen to hide himself and torment her with his presence.

She dismissed that, for that would be pretty severe behavior -- though not impossible, for elves can be great tricksters.

She yelled out, in the soft-edged tones of the elvin tongue, but got no reply. She called out again, and yet again, and even spoke the few words she knew of the brownies' much harder language, thinking (illogically) that the voice might belong to one of them. No luck. The voice remained. It was harsh and insistent; she deduced someone (or something) was *seeking* her. It was not a prankster's voice: it was a voice that dripped with danger.

On she went, her large, almond eyes seeking safety with growing difficulty in the dreary catacombs. Her light -- a blue phosphor stick -- served poorly to illuminate her path. But it was all she had.

The tunnel was narrow and cramped and foul-smelling. Elves like wide, open places, and plenty of fresh air, so this was doubly terrifying. Whatever it was that followed her... and it struck her, like a lightning bolt: it probably lived here. And if it lived here, there might be others!

The voice? It spoke admonishingly, telling her to go no further; that it wished to speak with her. That's all she could discern, for the language was crude, barbaric-sounding... just the kind of speech she would expect in such a horrid place. It didn't require much imagination to know what was being intended!

Oh, how she rued her curiosity! So close to her birthday, too. She did not have elf powers yet; she could not dispatch the voice with elvish powers. She had to outwit it.

She still had no idea where she was. She would go down a ways, then level off, rise a bit, and go down again. When she came to a junction in the tunnels she fretted -- but only for a few seconds. She quickly made up her mind, darting into the next tunnel, hoping that it was the one that would lead her back to the sunshine world and safety. Yet each time she decided, she only seemed to be deeper and deeper in the earth.

Jeni did not know how long she ran, or how far. She knew only that she was getting tired. Pursued or not, she was going to have to find an escape soon, or she would collapse.

Just as that thought grabbed hold of her, a shadow separated itself from a wall and sprang in front of her. Startled, she almost dropped her elf-light. The element of surprise worked to the shadow's advantage, and in seconds it had her by her long, golden hair and was pulling her unceremoniously toward its lair. Jeni screamed and struggled, but to no avail. She was too weak, and anyway her captor -- which she now saw was a dreaded ogre -- was far too powerful for her. Its gray-green hide was thick with muscles. Its toad-like mouth was filled with razor-sharp teeth that were made for tearing and rending flesh. The stories she had heard -- and they were unsubstantiated -- were that ogres lived deep within the earth, rising to the surface only at sunrise or sunset, to snatch their prey and drag it down to the depths, to devour at their pleasure.

She struggled, she squealed, even begged for mercy, but the ogre paid no attention. It continued to drag her along the rocky floor, a sickly hissing sound the only other sound that was present.

The end of the tunnel was in sight, and Jeni saw what awaited her. This was obviously the ogre's abode. Bones were scattered and heaped in piles, some of them with bits of meat still on them. The stench was overpowering. Jeni burst with a new surge of energy, but again to no avail. In a few minutes her own bones would mix with those before her. She began to cry.

Just as all seemed lost, another shadow appeared. The elf-light, which she still held fast in her right hand, was knocked away. It fell to the floor and was extinguished. It was now pitch black.

The appearance of a second creature was enough for the ogre to let go of her. She took advantage of the opportunity by getting quickly to her feet and running back the way she had come. In the dark, she had no sense of obstacles, but she did not care. It was enough that she was free.

Behind her the ogre and the second creature were very loud. Thuds and the scraping of feet and howls of pain and all manner of pushing and shoving and striking echoed in the dark. But Jeni did not intend to wait around to see which one emerged victorious. There was no guarantee that *both* creatures weren't interested in making a meal of her!

So she ran, stumbled, bounced against the earthen walls, fell, ran some more. Her progress was wretched, but at least she was getting away. Then the fighting ceased and it got very quiet. Jeni stopped her running, and her breathing, and listened. Nothing. She stretched her fine elvish ears; she waited. And then... there was a slow-moving noise, feet crunching on gravel. The victor was making its wait toward her!

She almost panicked. She couldn't outrun a creature in its own habitat, so she decided to go still, to cozy herself up against a wall, making herself as small as possible, in the hope that her pursuer would not notice her and go away.

She waited. And waited. And waited. And just when she was sure she had escaped a heinous fate... the creature in the dark reached out and clasped her with two powerful hands.

She screamed; she struggled. What now had her was not the ogre - for ogres don't have hands - but it was very strong. Resistance was pointless.

"Don't struggle," said a voice.

She stopped, caught by surprise. *Don't struggle? What kind of thing is that for a monster to say?*

"Don't struggle," the voice repeated, more pleasantly now. "I'm a friend."

Friend? Jeni's confusion struggled to find its way into words.

"I didn't save you from that ogre in order to hurt you," the voice continued. "I've been trying to help you all along."

Jeni was still too frightened to comprehend. *Save me? Friend?* With an effort she asked, "What do you mean: you've tried to help me?"

The voice... which was clearly male... answered.

"I tried to warn you at the tunnel's entrance, and for quite some time thereafter. I yelled at you, but you didn't hear."

"You were yelling at me? I didn't know. Besides, your words are strange to me. I... I thought you were a monster!"

The voice laughed, a small laugh so as not to give offense. Jeni wished she had her elf-light so she could *see* her rescuer. But save for the faintest silhouette in the dark she had no idea what he looked like.

"Well, next time," he replied, "you'll listen a little better!"

"I don't understand," she countered. "Who... what are you?"

"All in good time," was the response. "For the moment, just think of me as a friend."

Jeni said nothing. Instead, she listened as her rescuer explained that he would lead her to safety, if she just stayed close.

She obeyed. Along the way she couldn't help but ask questions, sprinkled here and there with remarks concerning her gratitude.

"My people," he answered, "have lived below the surface for many generations. It has become our home. It is also the home of the ogre, and we have always dreaded him, for he has taken a number of us for his food -- until today. I thank you, in behalf of my people, for helping us finally be rid of him."

"But why do you live here?" she asked.

"We live here because we must."

"Why don't you live in the world above?"

"We did, long ago, so say our storytellers. We lived in your world, but were forced to come down here."

"Forced? You mean by some other creatures?"

"Some other creatures... Funny you should put it that way. Yes, I guess they were. They were us... ourselves."

"I don't understand...."

"Our legends are not clear, but we were visited by some terrible peril, and as a consequence we fled, first into caves, and then into tunnels we dug from the caves, until we had an entire network of them, in which we have built our world."

The shock had a double impact on Jeni, for it occurred to her that her rescuer must be from that race of creatures that were considered long dead.

"Anyway," he continued, "we tunneled and dug our way into the earth, waiting for better times so that we could return to the surface. Only the longer we stayed, the more our bodies and senses became attuned to the dark. Now, it would be impossible for us to return, for our eyes would not permit it."

"Yet you are strong, and brave," she sputtered. "My people would welcome you."

"If only that were true," her rescuer sighed. "I think not. We have watched from afar for many years, from the shadows, from places you did not know. I don't think your people would share dominion with such as we."

"I don't believe that!"

"No? Your people are the masters of the sunshine world, are they not? Yours alone possess the magics and the powers that separate you from the other folk. It would not be the same. Trust me; you would not welcome us."

Minutes later they came to that same opening that had begun Jeni's adventure. In the bright sunlight she was able to see her rescuer. He was not very different from her own people, save for the fact that he didn't have pointed ears. He was her height, but pale -- strikingly so. And the eyes: she couldn't see his eyes, for he was shielding them from the light that was too bright for him. It was clear that he would not be going any further. She stopped and faced him.

"I don't even know your name," she said.

The other turned his head slightly and answered. "I am Ren. Don't worry about me or my people. We'll be all right. Though it would be nice if I could see you again."

Jeni touched his hand gently with her own and nodded.

"I'd like that. May I come here again -- perhaps some evening?"

"That would be nice. When it is dark you might be able to see more of us. Yes, that would be nice."

"You're wrong about us," she said. "We would share our world with you."

"But for one thing," said Ren. "You forget: we cannot see in your world. Our eyes are too weak."

It was Ren's turn to be wrong. Still, she promised she'd return. Minutes later she waved goodbye and was on her way home, smug in the knowledge that she knew what magic she would ask the elders to give her for her eleventh birthday. It would be an unusual request, but elf law said it must be granted. Then, she would use that magic to help Ren and his people -- by giving them the ability to see the beauty and the brilliance of her world. It was the least she could do to repay him for saving her life.

She was so filled with joy at what she proposed that she hadn't even remembered to ask Ren about the plaque and the funny marks that had drawn her to his world in the first place. It was just as well; doubtless Ren would not be able to explain to her or any-one else the meaning of the words:

FALLOUT SHELTER

12.

The last story was the most puzzling, and led all three to be glad, on the one hand, that it *was* the last one. On the other hand, though, there was an unspoken hope that *more* of these old stories would be found. Once again, there was that daunting question: "What is man?"

"*Hesperius*"

The Scribe sat dumbfounded at his discovery. It was late at night and autumn winds were pitching the branches of an elder maple violently against the windowpanes of the tiny scriptorum. It was the signal that a thunderstorm was approaching from the west. Hesperius, however, was too engrossed in his labors to pay it much heed.

He was lost in his work, hunched over a fragile manuscript that had found its way to him earlier in the day, the offering of a traveler who had begged a meal of cheese and mead. The wrinkled parchment was unrequested payment.

"It's not much," said the traveler, "but it's all I have, save for the rags upon my back and a trace of gold in one of my teeth. Take it, so that I may sleep more honestly for your offer of hospitality."

At first, he refused the gift. He felt uneasy about taking anything from his bedraggled visitor. But the other kept insisting, and so, not wishing to offend, he accepted it.

Now, many hours after the traveler had departed, Hesperius sat and stared at the treasure that lay before him.

And it *was* a treasure, at least to him, for it spoke of something that he - and many others before him - had thought about and pondered for years: the origins of his people, where they came from, and where most of them had gone.

All of this from a mere vagabond, a ragamuffin lad who had appeared out of nowhere on an otherwise indifferent afternoon. He stretched his mind to remember how it had happened, and was both surprised and angry that he could not. The traveler -- was he young or old? He'd exchanged pleasantries with Hesperius about the weather and the harvest, while consuming ladles of water that he primed from an ancient well. The traveler's appearance? Once again, memory failed, and he cursed into the window. How could he forget what a man looked like who had supped with him scant hours ago? Short, tall, round, thin; nothing clicked.

Extremely odd, he mumbled into his snow-white beard, especially considering how few people he had contact with, up here, on his mountain. When was the last time he had *had* a visitor? Once again, an imperfect memory failed.

The winds were now furious enough to be competing for his attention, and for the first time he looked up from his desk to see and hear the tap-tapping of snake-like branches on the window. He tried to ignore it, willing himself to concentrate on the mysterious traveler and the document. Minutes later he threw up his hands in defeat. It was useless, he grumbled in the increasing din. *Nothing* registered. So he sat there, frustrated and confused.

An hour later, the storm still had not arrived, so he turned his attention back to the parchment. He craned against the flickering light of a lone tapered candle. It wasn't easy. The ravages of time -- for the parchment was old -- had served to obscure and obliterate a number of words, even whole passages. Ignorance served to invalidate the rest of it: words Hesperius did not know; an occasional phrase he could not comprehend. And yet: the text looked familiar...

But the *flow* of the document -- if "document" was the right word -- excited him like nothing he had ever experienced. There was the mention of a place -- somewhere near a river in the East -- with landmarks highlighted. Some others, he cursed, were blurred and incomprehensible, beyond which only guesses could be made. It was not enough: this *must* be verified, and the only way to do that was to leave: to go east, to locate the landmarks, and find ... what?

That was a historian's great purpose -- and Hesperius thought of himself as such (much mocked and maligned by those with whom he came into contact [when was the last time?], in a day and age when most people shunned *any* reminder of their past). He had to prove the parchment's validity -- or its *in*validity -- and as soon as possible. Winter was coming; in another month snow and biting cold would be his boon companion. If he were to get the answers to his questions he'd have to do it now.

Then he sat back and sighed. The Elderfolk; the Ones of Legend: these were things his grandfather had told him about when he was a youngster. And his grandfather's grandfather. They were tantalizing stories, all passed on by word of mouth. Myths, more than likely, but valued all the same, especially by the young, in their hunger for something new.

Hesperius was well past his childhood, and in fact was into the winter of his life. His grandfather had been gone for many years. Yet the stories were still there, sitting on the edge of memory. Now, as if possessed by a demonic urge, he felt compelled to seek out their source.

At that instant, the first blast of the anticipated storm hit with a fury, and he looked up from his desk at the rain that was cascading thunderously against the window.

The next morning did not show overmuch nature's violent display of the night before. A few quiet puddles here and there bore silent testimony to the passage of the deluge.

By mid-morning Hesperius was packed and ready to go. He surveyed his surroundings one last time. There wasn't much to see: a dilapidated, ramshackle wood-framed house, a few spent rows of corn and tomatoes (he'd already harvested most of them), and a hazy view of the blue-gray hills and valley below. A played-out farmstead; not even any chickens or pigs. Just a poor piece of dirt on top of brittle clay. Nothing to be missed, surely, and save for the pitiful pile of planking that for years had served as home and shelter, nothing that would command anyone's interest as a dwelling.

His knapsack packed, a hefty knife strapped to his belt for food and protection, the parchment pressed into his leather breeches, he started down the mountain.

By mid-afternoon, Hesperius had begun to doubt the wisdom of his quest. By dusk, he was all but convinced he had no business rambling about the countryside. His feet were killing him; he was nicked about the face and ankles from a couple of clumsy falls; he had lost at least an hour from literally going around in circles... and he was bone-tired. On top of that, he found that he'd forgotten to pack any flint, so he cursed himself for not being able to coax a fire to warm himself and to cook his victuals. Thoroughly spent, his aches and pains finally got the better of him, and he curled himself into a hollow spot in some tall weeds and fell gratefully into sleep.

His slumber was not an easy one. It was pock-marked with dark imaginings, little splotches here and there of things both familiar and bizarre. His dream self showed his home, more comfortable and attractive than it really was, complete with a stable of cows and a clutch of chickens. In a blink, there was the same scene, this time desolate, with a single stone marker where the non-existent cows and chickens had congregated. A lone figure stared down at it, but he couldn't tell who it was. Shadows kept him from seeing what was inscribed upon the stone.

The dream shifted, to a long, lush plain, bristling with yellowed grasses and healthy evergreens. In the middle of a meadow was a girl. He could only see her from behind, but his dream self suggested she was someone he knew. She stood there, very quietly, holding a single flower in a cupped right hand.

In a flash, there was a city, the likes of which he had never seen, or even imagined. It was an exotic place, of bright and extra-ordinary design. Then the dreams repeated, this time with subtle changes, until at last he was back in his own house.

Deep melancholia took him over. *Nocturnal doddering of a silly old man,* he sighed. *And a fool! Traipsing about the countryside at your age! And for what? A few scribbles on a parchment. Has life become* that *boring?*

That may have been the answer: he *was* an old and lonely man, who last had tasted summer's fire more years ago than he could recall. It's better, part of him argued, to be active -- even if the act may be foolish -- than to just hunker down and wait for death.

For that is precisely what he had been doing. The thought shocked him, for until this moment he'd not realized it. Now, thanks to an enigmatic visit, he had a reason... to live? Even if the ventur-ing forth was dangerous - and at his age it most certainly *was* - it would give his life more meaning than anything he had done... in how many years?

So it wasn't the "historian" in him that compelled him to under-take this adventure: that was just an excuse. The *reason* was much more personal.

Hah! he grumbled to himself, not trusting his words to be heard by the birds or the foxes or any of the other critters who by chance were nearby. *I'm not only an old fool, but a crazy one, as well!* But that did not change his mind, or his purpose. He kept on with his journey.

Three days and uncountable miles later Hesperius had found none of the landmarks hinted at on the parchment. Nor was he any longer sure of his directions. Go east... but by what path? He had selected it arbitrarily. Was he taking the right one? Such questions were tearing at him, as exhaustion and myriad aches and pains were taking him over. *Stupid!* he yammered. And scared: he had come this far (however "far" that was) and were he to decide to end this nonsense and go home right now, he wasn't even sure how to do it. He had not looked back once to see where he'd been; he'd not noted even one tree or rock formation so that he could retrace his footsteps.

Stupid! his mind shouted at him. His body also shouted at him. *Too much pain! Too much pain!*

At the end of that third day, he stopped. Shoulders shrugged, the pain of his efforts now so great that he could hardly move, he knew that he could go no further. He collapsed, in a heap, beside some bushes and fell into a deep sleep.

He dreamed the same dreams, but with predictable additions and subtractions. The girl was still there, smiling at him, reaching out to him. She said nothing, but she didn't have to. In the dream, he clasped her youthful hand, and together they walked through a thick grove of trees, a bright shining seeming to envelop them. They came upon that strange stone, and stopped to look at it. But his dream self still would not reveal what was written upon it. Then the two of them walked away, hand in hand, until they were out of sight. There were no aches and pains, only perfect health and a future with each other.

As he awakened into the all-consuming brightness of a new day, Hesperius was glad he had made this trip. It had revivified him, had re-energized his intellect, had...

He stopped, for in his reflections he became aware of something that jolted him. He looked down, and saw that even though he'd been traveling for many days his knapsack still contained the same amount of food and water he'd left home with. And the map? *What map?* He hadn't looked at it since... the night of the storm. He hadn't brought it with him.

How could that be? What does it mean? And then, something else tugged at him. The dreams. They were so clear, so sharply defined. Had he ever had dreams like those before? *No,* was the response that slipped through his teeth like a forbidden word.

There had never been dreams like those.

He noticed something else. He wasn't in any pain. The nicks and scratches... they weren't there. *But they were real... weren't they?*

Finally, almost as an afterthought, he had the answer. And strangely enough, it didn't frighten him. Instead, he looked up, saw the young woman of his dream. Only she was real. She stood on the crest of a ridge, no more than a hundred yards ahead, and was smiling at him. Hesperius knew that together they would get the answers to all of his questions. For the first time in years, he didn't feel so old.

epilogue

For one last time, the three goblin scholars sat around the table, reflecting on their investigations.

"So," announced Nicomaides with no preamble whatsoever, "what have we learned?"

"We've learned that we can survive some rather daffy stories." The sarcasm was Tal's, and was not unexpected.

"There have been some good points raised," rebutted Serri, ever the optimist.

"Honor was a frequent theme," she added, "plus integrity, humor, respect, and doing the right thing."

"Even if it meant lying?" sneered Tal.

"Serri is right, but so is Tal," announced Nicomaides. "Lying is a terrible thing, and rarely helpful. Only once, in these stories, have we seen the exception to that rule."

"And courage?"

"We've seen fine examples of courage," said Nicomaides. "Some were obvious, some were not, but all led to positive endings."

"We've also seen love," added Serri. "Love for one's family, friends, and clan."

Tal harrumphed.

"We've also seen despair, which to my way of looking at things is more realistic."

"Agreed," answered Nicomaides. "Despair visits each of us more often than we would like, and frequently does not lend itself to a happy ending."

"Nevertheless," responded Serri, "we read stories that were mostly uplifting. Many of them I would like to read again."

"Some of what we read were just plain *preposterous*," countered Tal. "Creatures of metal, beings that could be something else...really, now!"

That, naturally, was the cue for Nicomaides to chime in, as he now did, with his "big picture" speech. Tal should have known he'd do that. He just glared.

"I think," the elder continued, "that in these twelve stories we have seen just about everything - good *and* bad - to which goblins can relate. Some of the *presentations* may have seemed alien, but the lessons they contained were not."

"What then remains?" asked Serri.

"An excellent question, and one which I see on Tal's face, too. As I see it, the stories need to be studied further, in conjunction with other scholars who can provide fresh opinions and insights.

"We need also to keep searching for new stories and fragments. Surely, there must be parchments yet undiscovered that will shed light on what we have read, and determined."

"Do you think there *are* other stories?" asked Serri.

"I do, indeed," answered Nicomaides. "It seems most unlikely that this batch, wonderful treasure that it is, constitutes the only existing remnant of the civilization or civilizations that produced it."

"And if we *do* find other stories?" asked Tal.

"Then," said Nicomaides, "we will stand a better chance at understanding the authors' true intent. Perhaps, too, it will help us understand the meaning of our *own* civilization."